Sam, Maddie,
and the
Mirror Dragon

Two inspired teens and their quest to
discover Mother Earth's secrets

Elizabeth Flanders
with Evan Prichard

SAM, MADDIE, AND THE MIRROR DRAGON

Two inspired teens
and their quest to discover
Mother Earth's secrets

Published by Flanders Teaching Tools
P.O. Box 1658, Ocean Park, Washington 98640
Paperback ISBN: 979-8-218-25894-8
eBook ISBN: 979-8-218-25895-5

Illustrations by Naeshi and by Evan Prichard
With Afterword by Mare Cromwell and Pam Montgomery
Cover and book design by Jess LaGreca, Mayfly book design

Library of Congress Catalog Number: 2023914829
First Printing: 2023

Attempts are being made to secure permission from the various copyright holders and sources mentioned in this book. If you are a copyright holder and feel your rights have been infringed, please contact us at the above address, or MirrorDragon@ yahoo.com and let us know.

Publisher's Cataloging-in-Publication Data
provided by Five Rainbows Cataloging Services
Names: Flanders, Elizabeth. | Pritchard, Evan, 1955- | Hilger, Anne-Sophie, illustrator.
Title: Sam, Maddie, and the mirror dragon : two inspired teens and their quest to discover Mother Earth's secrets / Elizabeth Flanders.
Description: Ocean Park, WA : Flanders Teaching Tools, 2023. | Summary: Two inspired teens and their quest to discover Mother Earth's secrets. | Audience: Grades 4 to 7.
Identifiers: ISBN 979-8-218-25894-8 (paperback) | ISBN 979-8-218-25895-5 (ebook)
Subjects: LCSH: Illustrated works. | CYAC: Magic--Fiction. | Dragons--Fiction. | Ecology--Fiction. | Animal communication. | Northwest, Pacific--Juvenile fiction. | BISAC: JUVENILE FICTION / Magical Realism. | JUVENILE FICTION / Science & Nature / Environment. | JUVENILE FICTION / Visionary & Metaphysical. | JUVENILE FICTION / Fantasy / Dragons, Unicorns & Mythical Creatures.
Classification: LCC PZ7.1.F63 2023 (print) | LCC PZ7.1.F63 (ebook) | DDC [Fic]--dc23.

DEDICATION

I dedicate this book to my grandson Steven and to all the young people, born and unborn, who carry new life-giving stories for our world. May their parents, teachers, and mentors support their gifts, allowing them to grow into who they were created to be.

Elizabeth Flanders

SAM, MADDIE, AND THE MIRROR DRAGON

Two inspired teens
and their quest to discover
Mother Earth's secrets

SAM AND THE MOTHER TREE

It's a sunny fall afternoon, rare in the Pacific Northwest. In Sam's area, most of the trees have already been cleared for new housing developments but behind the field near his home are several acres of beautiful old-growth forest, miraculously spared the axe. Sam is outside playing soccer in the huge field—a spot he loves. Today the air smells like fresh spring rain to him. Other kids are playing on the same grounds; however, since it is as large as a football field, he feels he has lots of open space to himself. He's been watching soccer videos for pointers lately and is practicing his footwork and is especially having trouble learning the swerve kick to make the ball bend to the left off his right instep. It is just one of the kicks he hopes to master before the upcoming game—the first game of the season. Without warning, a swirling wind captures his ball and sends it speeding towards the forest in a bending arc, curling to the left. He races after the ball, half fascinated by the sudden swirling wind and half afraid of losing the ball. "What's creating this vortex?" he wonders. A vortex is a mass of swirling air or fluid, like a whirlwind, whirlpool, or tornado; he learned that last year in science class, but this is a new kind of vortex, one he didn't know existed, an invisible one.

The ozone smell of freshly fallen rain gets stronger as he steps in among the trees. He spots his ball perched beside a cluster of sword ferns growing against the trunk of the large Oregon white oak, a native of the Pacific Northwest. Sam thinks of his grandmother. She's a naturalist, and while he's more interested in soccer, computer games, and his friends, he remembers the excitement in her voice when she identified that tree. He can almost hear her say, "Look Sam, see the rounded protrusions on this leaf? It's called a lobed leaf. Look at the furrows and ridges on its light gray bark!" He does enjoy being alone in nature with his grandmother. Her love for the natural world is infectious.

A black salamander with a gold stripe down its back slithers through the grass by his foot, then heads right for the Oregon white oak and jumps playfully on top of his soccer ball and stands for a moment with its neck pivoting as if guarding the tree, or perhaps an imaginary soccer net, then jumps away like an acrobat. Sam has a flashback to a wonderful May day four years ago with Nana, his grandmother. Nana took him on a backyard safari to hunt for salamanders. He can hear her "teacher" voice saying, "See the black salamander with the fancy gold racing stripe? It's our own Western long-toed salamander. The scientific name is Ambystoma macrodactylum; in other words, an amphibian with long fingers."

"WOW!" Exclaimed Sam. "Terradactyl? Is he a dinosaur? I thought they went extinct."

"No, he's not even a reptile, but an amphibian and, like many dinosaurs, can live on land or in water. His kind goes back to the Mesozoic era."

Sam blurts out, "He looks like a miniature dragon. Look at that long tail! Can I touch it?"

Nana extends her hand over the salamander and says, "Better not! Its skin excretes a mild toxin, and if you licked your hand afterwards, you might get a stomach ache."

He looks around with his grandmother's eyes and sees

wild roses and orange trumpet honeysuckle growing nearby.

"Oh, the honeysuckle smells just so delicious!" she would say.

"Nana seems to know all the plants and animals personally," Sam thinks to himself. "I wish I could be like that." Sam spots a green darner dragonfly as it lights on a flower. I can hear Nana say, "Green darning dragonfly: our Washington State insect! Named dragonfly because of its grey-green iridescent wings, its long neck, and its Paleozoic genealogy. But her friends call her Anax junius."[1]

"Nana says you will migrate south in September," Sam says to the attentive insect, not expecting a response.

MOTHER TREE

As he reaches down to recover his ball, something quite unexpected happens. He finds himself inside the vortex. His feet grow roots into the rich forest soil, and he feels himself getting taller and taller until it feels like his head is touching the sky. "Welcome to the Inner World," he hears inside his mind. "Hmm. Those words. They're inside my mind! But I didn't put them there. Who did?" he wonders.

"I did!" answers a mysterious, disembodied voice, suddenly clearer, but echoing as if from the bottom of a well, "I am the Mother Tree. Welcome to the Inner World," she responds telepathically.

"Er—Who are you?" he asks with a curiosity that is both scientific and philosophic in nature.

As the vortex subsides and Sam returns to his 14-year-old size, he notices his senses are sharpened. The light shimmers and sparkles, and he can identify all the scents wafting through the air at once, mushrooms, moss, and honeysuckle. Each scent is distinctive, yet he is experiencing them in the same instant. The same begins to happen with sounds. He hears the leaves moving in the trees, a woodpecker tapping a rhythm on a stump, songbirds each singing their own sweet song, a raccoon chittering in the distance, and the high-pitched bark of a coyote, each playing on the same wildly tuned harp in the same moment.

"You're called—uh—*Mother*?"

"Yes, oh curious one, Creator has given me this role. Two hundred species of flora and fauna depend on me for their survival. I gift my acorns to deer, gray squirrels, red squirrels, chipmunks, wild turkeys, crows, flying squirrels, rabbits, opossums, blue jays, quail, raccoons, and wood ducks, just to name a few. I also provide homes for hollow-nesting bird species and small mammals. Just don't get me started on the vast universe of life teeming in the soil around my roots—rhizomes, fungi, insects, and much more. Have you ever had a conversation with a Palouse earthworm?"[2]

"Wow! My grandmother would love to meet you!"

"We have met, young friend. There's a lot you don't know about your grandmother. I suggest you ask her about her travels."

"I sure will," answers Sam, intrigued.

"I have a gift for you, too, but not an acorn! Acorns are seeds of the future from my terrestrial connections. This gift is from my celestial connections. I am a pillar of energy connecting the earth and sky into one complete whole. My branches are pathways to the stars, some of them just burning to be wished upon, especially the falling ones. Are you ready to reach for your dream?"

"I don't know," Sam pauses to think—so many questions! "But I can't be late for dinner. Mother'll be worried."

"No worries. The Inner World exists in the eternal NOW where time does not exist. When you leave here it will be the same time you entered. Best you go now, however. Look under the sword fern cluster and you will find your gift, a crystal. It is your key to the Inner World. Go now, consider all you have experienced, and if you are up for an adventure, come back with the crystal."

When Sam steps out of the forest, he checks his watch—no time has passed. He runs home, cradling his soccer ball in his left arm, as the crystal in his right pocket bumps gently against his thigh.

"Yum," he says as he smells sesame chicken upon entering the kitchen door, one of his favorite meals. A moment later, he learns even more good news. His grandmother is here. "Nana!" he yells as he runs to give her a big bear hug, which surprises them both since he doesn't hug much anymore. He's growing up, almost as tall as Nana now. She is in her usual uniform— jeans with a colorful T-shirt. Nana especially loves African and South American prints; her closet is full of them! She usually wears crystal and stone necklaces and bracelets, too, and she's wearing turquoise today. Nana's white hair falls in ringlets around her face, and her blue eyes shine in response to the hug.

"Awesome T-shirt, Nana. Where'd you get it?"

"I got it when I lived in Africa," Nana replies. "African prints are so colorful. Merchants bring them to open air markets, and you barter for what you want. Then you take the material to a tailor, who usually works in a small hut with one sewing machine."

"Wow! I'm down for hearing more about your life in Africa, Nana," Sam exclaims. "Are you staying for dinner?"

"No, Sam, but we will find a time."

"Did you have fun?" his mother asks.

"Oh yeah! I practiced my footwork and spent some chill time in the forest. Did you know the Oregon white oak supports 200 species of flora and fauna?"

"Wow! Who told you that?" she responds.

"The tree." The words slip from his lips before he can think.

A deep belly laugh erupts from his mother. "You're a real comedian, Sam. You can always make me laugh." Nana, on the other hand, raises her eyebrows the way she does when intrigued and gives him a knowing look, but says nothing.

Sam sometimes imagines his mother, Sarah, as a whirling dervish, dancing around the kitchen with boundless energy, picking herbs from her window garden, her red curls falling over her sky-blue eyes, just like Nana's. It's not unusual for her to be talking on the phone as well. She is president both of Uplift, a community thrift store, and the Parent Teacher Association at his school. She has created an army of tutors to support at-risk readers. She explains, to anyone willing to listen, that by third grade, children need to have learned to read so they can read to learn. Her army of volunteers has raised the percentage of third graders reading at grade level from 50% to 70% and climbing. People say, "When Sarah comes around, get ready to work!"

Dinner is delicious, as always; afterwards Sam meets his friends online to play Fortnite. Every now and then he feels the crystal warm up against his thigh and wonders about all that he has experienced.

Sam and the Mirror Dragon

As he is preparing for bed, Sam takes the crystal from his pocket and once again smells fresh spring rain. "Hmmm!" He feels it heating up in the palm of his hand, as it did earlier in his pocket. Within it, an image momentarily becomes visible, a sparkling silver dragon; then just as quickly dissolves. "Must have imagined that," he thinks, as he puts the crystal under his pillow and quickly falls to sleep.

In his dream, he climbs onto the silver dragon's back. They fly together, and the dragon introduces him to the stars. He remembers the dream when he awakens, but quickly forgets it as he gets ready for school. It's a busy Friday ahead. He forgets the crystal under his pillow as well.

When he gets home that evening, he has a quick dinner and goes to his room to do his homework. When he steps into his room, he pauses as he smells fresh spring rain once again; then puts his attention on his homework. The work goes more easily than usual. He feels like he is flying through the pages. That night he dreams again.

He is standing beside the white oak tree. He faces a being known as Owl looking out from a hollow in Mother's trunk. Owl has beautiful white, silver, and gold feathers and a heart-shaped face. Owl's dark piercing eyes deliver a message to Sam's mind.

"Sam, are you willing to keep your promise?"

"Huh? What promise?"

"The promise you made to Creator before you were born."

"How'm I supposed to remember *that?*"

"By stepping out of time."

Then Sam wakes up. He feels the crystal humming under his pillow and, still half asleep, gets dressed. He absent-mindedly puts the crystal in his jeans leg pocket and zips it up. It's Saturday, and he feels a pull to the soccer field. He has a quick breakfast, tells his mother where he is going, grabs his soccer ball, and runs out the door. As he walks, his mind is filled with his usual obsession—becoming his team's captain and wearing a captain's golden armband. He knows he needs to improve his playing and leadership skills if he is going to have a shot at that dream. The next game is a week away. He knows practicing alone is very different than playing in a real game. Sam knows he gets nervous under game-time pressure.

When he reaches the field, the pull strengthens and he finds himself in the forest, by the ferns at the base of the Oregon white oak tree. Immediately, he is carried by the energy vortex into the Inner World, even as his eyes continue to see the "real" world.

"Mother Tree, Owl came in my dream last night and asked if I was willing to keep the promise I made to Creator before I was born. How the heck should I know?"

"Ah, leave it to Owl to get right to the point. However, that question can take a lifetime to answer. Do you want to know the promise you made before you were born?"

"I don't know! What is the promise! Why am I being asked *now*?"

"Because now you can hear me. I have gifts to guide those who can travel to the Inner World. The journey is packed with adventures! It's filled with awe and wonder; however, it does take courage. The question is, are you willing to take the leap?"

Again, the Western long-toed salamander appears, standing on a white quartzite rock. He takes a leap and disappears into the tall grass. But was he "real" or a dream? As Sam reflects on all that has occurred, he notices the light changing. A subtle silver sparkle in the air becomes brighter. Suddenly, a brilliant flash forms into a sparkling dragon reflecting the rainbow colors of the surrounding forest. Her eyes, glowing

SILVERLIGHT

orbs, are a kaleidoscope of changing colors. Her neck is like a glittering staircase, her feet like eagles' claws, but the most distinctive feature of this powerful being is that each scale is like a mirror into a dream. Sam senses a vortex of love emanating from the dragon, which reminds him of his mother's and grandmother's love.

"I am the Mirror Dragon SilverLight, my son. I am your guide inward, but only if you choose."

Sam loves SilverLight immediately. He thinks of his mother and grandmother. He knows he is fortunate to have his parents and grandparents. They are always there for him, supporting his interests. Not all of his friends are so fortunate. SilverLight seems like part of his family already.

"Yes, I choose YES!" and as he says these words, Sam feels an energetic cord connect his heart to SilverLight's. "I met you in my dream, didn't I? We flew to the stars."

"Oh yes, we all come from the stars, you know."

"Yeah, I knew that! In science class I just read something from a planetary scientist named Dr. Ashley King. He said it is really true. Most of the elements in the human body were made in the stars and came to earth through supernova explosions. How cool is that!"

"Yes, but can astrophysicists explain why millions of people wish upon a star? Is it because stars remind them of something beyond themselves? Something greater?" SilverLight asks. "Some 10,000 years ago people all over North America were doing ceremony in conjunction with the annual Perseid meteor showers, in other words, falling stars. Many ceremonial landscapes from that time have survived that are aligned with

Perseus, the constellation from which these meteors seem to come from 330 degrees on the northwest horizon.[3] Were they wishing on those stars? Hmmm, I don't know, I wasn't born yet, but I'd bet some of them were."

Sam is silent for a while; then asks, "I'm confused, Silver-Light. I see your silver scales, like mirrors reflecting the colors and shapes of the forest, but sometimes it's like you are occupying the same space as the trees and bushes. Are you?"

"Yes, Sam, your perception is correct. I am in the same space, but in another dimension. Everything is made of energy, vibrating atoms, and molecules. I am simply vibrating at a different frequency than the forest. Are you up for an adventure this morning? A fall storm with gale-force winds is developing in our area, and I want to take a look."

Without a second thought, Sam jumps on SilverLight's back near her neck and they take off. Sam feels his stomach lurch the way it does during carnival rides. As he feels SilverLight leveling out, he has the sense of moving through a tunnel at warp speed. When SilverLight emerges into the atmosphere above Mother Earth, Sam sees a web of shimmering light filaments connecting points of light against a black background.

He wonders what this web is, and SilverLight answers telepathically. "Scientists call this the Cosmic Web. It is the energetic structure that holds the universe together. I call it the Net of Love, for what humans think of as the "All" was originally created out of something much greater, love. Love is the most powerful force in the universe. It connects all the galaxies and universes; all of them—vortices, whirlpools of light, matter, gases, and cosmic dust, all reflecting the nature of love through their flowing motion. However, in this moment, we are only seeing the energetic grid around Mother Earth."

"You can hear my thoughts, SilverLight?"

"Yes, Sam, our minds have merged. We are One."

THE STORM VORTEX

"I see areas where the shimmering lights aren't visible, SilverLight. There, I only see dark clouds. How did they get there?"

"Everything is energy, Sam. As Albert Einstein once said, 'Energy cannot be created or destroyed, but it can be converted from one form to another.' For instance, water evaporates into the air when heated and freezes into ice when cold. It's the law of thermodynamics. Human emotions are energy too. Have you ever walked into a room and known something was wrong? Well, there is something wrong on a planetary scale. There is far too much judgment, hatred, greed, fear, rage, destruction, and violence in the human collective right now, and you are seeing the effects on the Cosmic Web."

"Come on, are we dinky little humans that powerful?"

"Such things are hard to prove scientifically, but we can easily see the links in the chain between destructive emotions and destructive actions and how those actions affect the surrounding ecosphere time after time. Just look around you. Human beings are not the only force in play. There are many planetary and galactic forces that are totally independent of humans.

However, Creator has given a potentially powerful role to you folks on earth, and you are responsible for handling that power carefully. Some humans have accepted this responsibility, but many haven't yet. As a result, nature's elemental forces have taken matters into their own hands, and you will see why. See the eye-in-that-storm-vortex developing? This storm will hit your area tonight. Batten down the hatches, as they say! Hold on tight, we're going in! I want you to experience the full power of this storm—there is something in the middle I want you to see."

Suddenly Sam feels them flying in a counterclockwise circle moving inwards. Round and round they fly in smaller and smaller circles, picking up enormous speed along the way until they enter the eye of the storm, where all is quiet. Sam is quite dizzy. He hears SilverLight whisper, "Remember, Sam, there is quiet in the middle of every storm." Sam has a few moments to catch his breath, before they travel back out through widening circles at slower speeds, until they exit all together.

"You need to let go, Sam, so you can invite in your soul level experiences more easily. When you tighten in fear, you work against the flow and make it harder for yourself. Relax, accept, and trust, become One with the positive energy currents in your life and you will receive what you need."

"What's so frigging positive about this storm? It'll blow trees down, cause flooding, and leave us without power. Without internet! I hate these storms! I hate the wind!"

"Look at the grid, Sam," and as he does, he sees the gale-force winds blowing away the dark clouds which were obstructing the cosmic web, leaving the grid lights shimmering.

"Yes," SilverLight continues, as she nods her majestic head. "Nature's elemental weather forces will protect Mother Earth and the structure of Creation from destructive choices. We can help if we are willing. However, we need to get you back now to help your family prepare for the storm. You can reach me anytime by holding the crystal in your palm and saying my name."

They travel back through the tunnel at warp speed and suddenly Sam finds himself standing by the White oak tree, the crystal in his palm. He puts the crystal in the thigh pocket of his jeans, zips it up, and runs home. "The winds are really picking up!" he thinks.

His father is in the yard when Sam arrives. They are both panting a bit. "Oh good. Sure am relieved to see you back home. You know there is a storm brewing, a lollapalooza! Finish putting all the lawn furniture and potted plants in the garage! I'll go help your mom get out the hand-cranked radio, battery-powered lanterns, and flashlights!"

Sam's dad, Frank, is tall and lanky. He looks like a university professor with his herringbone glasses, but when he is doing physical work, his carved muscles pop out. Frank usually has a twinkle in his eye, but if he doesn't, watch out! He can become very intense when fighting injustices, whether supporting a bullied child or fighting an unjust law. Sam secretly calls his dad Justice Warrior, but never out loud, of course.

When he finishes placing the lawn furniture and potted plants safely in the garage, Sam goes in the kitchen door and finds his mom filling their large thermos with hot water. "I made sandwiches too. We'll keep 'em in the ice chest, so we don't have to open the fridge if the power goes out. Get your insulated underwear out where you can find it easily. You know storms in the Pacific Northwest can be cold!"

Once prepared, Sam's family sits down to a hot meal of spaghetti with meat sauce, garlic bread, and roasted vegetables. "Fill up, everyone, in case the power goes out," Mom advises. "Dad will hook up the generator, if necessary, but it's heavy to move and we don't need it if the outage isn't too long. After dinner, we need to close all the blinds and curtains to keep the heat in and flying debris out."

Residents of the Pacific Northwest are justly proud of their huge trees, but they can topple in high winds, damaging power lines. While these storms have always been common in Washington state, with climate change they are more intense, and are happening more often. It's important to be prepared for emergencies without power or phone service in these uncertain times. Sam's family understands and has practiced emergency drills.

That night, the house shakes. There is one thundering crash that Sam suspects is an uprooted tree, but it doesn't sound like it hits the house. In his mind's eye, Sam sees the clouds of dark human emotions dissipating, clearing the shimmering Cosmic Web, and says thank you to nature's elemental weather forces. He notices he relaxes when he says thank you.

Sam doesn't get much sleep that night and is tired in the morning, but also relieved. He sees the LED numbers on his clock and realizes the power is on. When he looks outside, he sees the tree he heard falling, which is now lying in the neighbor's yard. His dad is already outside helping the neighbor.

He's wearing his cut-resistant gloves and helmet and carrying his chainsaw. While appreciating his dad's muscles, Sam waves, and his dad yells, "Get some breakfast, then put on your work clothes and come help."

Mom has a big pot of oatmeal on the stove. Sam fills his bowl and adds brown sugar, cinnamon, and sliced bananas. "Yum," he thinks, "so warm and filling." Then he puts on his work clothes, drops the crystal into his side pocket, and zips it up.

Once outside, he sees his dad and the neighbor splitting the wood and cutting logs. Sam picks up the logs and piles them up where the firewood is kept. It's always sad to lose a tree, but there will be lots of logs for the fireplace next winter. As they are finishing up, the neighbor thanks them and offers to share the fireplace logs come winter. They shake hands.

MADDIE AND HER DOG SPARKS

Sam and his dad are hungry after all that work and return home. They are eating the sandwiches Mom prepared the night before when the phone rings. "Sure, I'll be right over, and I'll bring my son. He's a great help," his dad says and winks at Sam before hanging up.

"Sam, a co-worker has lost a tree too. He knows I have the right equipment and skills and needs help. Are you with me?"

"Sure, Dad," Sam replies. His dad is a good teacher, and Sam always learns a lot working with him. Besides, he just likes being by his side.

They jump in the truck. Dad slides their favorite CD into the car stereo, and they sing at the top of their lungs. When they arrive and climb out of the truck, Sam sees a mature big-leaf Maple tree, still holding its fall leaves, lying across the front yard. Broken potted plants lie underneath, and the tree has knocked out several slats of the fence. A girl his age is sitting by the felled tree with a white Miniature Schnauzer on her lap, and she is crying her eyes out. Sam recognizes her from school. She's his age but is in a different class. "Hi, Maddie."

"Where's your father?" Frank asks.

Maddie points to the garage door, while continuing to cry, as her dog gently licks her cheek. Sam sits down silently beside her. Maddie has brown hair and deep brown eyes. She's about as tall as Sam. Sam has strawberry blond hair and his mother's and grandmother's blue eyes. After a few minutes, Maddie begins to talk, in between sobs.

"Maple was my friend. No one understands. When I was sad, she lifted my spirits. When I had a problem, if I just sat under her quietly, an answer would come. I loved her, and I felt she loved me. What will I do without her?" she sobs.

Sam just sits quietly until her crying slows. "No one understands?" he asks.

"No one but Sparks here," she sobs as she hugs her dog. "My family laughs at me. They call me a tree hugger in a mean way and say a tree can't be a friend."

"I have a tree for a friend, but it is my secret."

"Really!?! I will keep your secret."

When Maddie's and Sam's fathers come out of the garage, they look at their children sitting on the ground and Sam's dad suggests, "Why don't you two take a walk. A change of scenery might help."

Maddie throws herself over the maple's trunk and quietly says, so only Sam can hear, "I love you, Maple. I will miss you so! Thanks for being my friend."

As they walk by the truck, Sam reaches into the glove compartment and takes out a pack of tissues. As he hands them to Maddie, he says, "I have someone I want you to meet. Let's go to the soccer field by my house." Sparks follows.

Maddie's new to their school this year, and Sam doesn't know her well, but he has been impressed with her courage and strength. When some tough guys cornered her, called her newbie, and tried to slap her, she quietly responded with some very effective martial arts moves. The boys winced and limped away.

As they continue walking, Maddie and Sparks move so quickly Sam has to push himself to keep up. When they reach the soccer field, Sam points to the forest. Maddie and Sparks are full-out running now, and Sam is a bit out of breath, but Maddie isn't out of breath at all. "Boy, is she strong! She's speeding up!" observes Sam.

As they enter the forest, Maddie sees a flame-skimmer dragonfly right at eye level, one of seventy-one sub-species of dragonflies in Washington State, possibly the most enchanting one of all, with its long red tail and its double set of golden wings. She comes to a dead stop. There is a fresh smell in the air and the light is shimmering. "Wow! I've been in here before, but this feels different. It's like a fairyland!" Sparks comes to alertness.[4]

"There *are* fairies here, dear Maddie, and much more, not to mention a few fire-breathing dragonflies. Welcome to the Inner World."

"Who is talking in my head?" Maddie wonders out loud as Sparks sniffs the ground, then looks up at a large tree. Suddenly a kaleidoscope of butterflies lands all over Sparks. One lands on his nose, and he looks cross-eyed at it with a goofy "I'm in love" smile on his face. Then a deer, chipmunk, raccoon, and wood duck amble through the brush and surround Sparks in the four directions, north, east, south, and west.

"I am speaking Maddie, and I see the animals have come to honor your Sparks. He is a healer."

This time Sam hears the Tree, too and smiles knowingly. Maddie says slowly, in disbelief, "... and you are ..."

"I am the Mother Tree here, and I have a message for you from your beloved Maple."

"You do?" Maddie starts sobbing again and pulls out the tissues Sam gave her, as Sparks and his entourage of adoring animals move closer to her. "How can I hear you? You're just a tree!"

"You are grieving, my love. When you are struck with loss, you stand on the threshold of the spirit world. Sorrow has opened your heart to be present in the moment—no past, no future, just presence and the capacity to listen within.[5] Beloved Maple wants you to know she isn't afraid of death the way humans are. She knows she will just change form. She also wants you to know you have the capacity to talk with other trees and plants. Not all want to talk to humans, so always ask permission first."

"How do you know what my Maple said?"

"We trees have vast underground communication networks, our wood-wide-web. Scientists call these mycorrhizal networks. Look it up! We are a great deal more alert, sociable, and intelligent than you think. We can alert other trees about danger—even if they are far away."[6]

After a long pause, Mother Tree says, "Look under the cluster of ferns at my base. There is a gift for you there." Maddie reaches down and brings up a small hollow bone, and Sparks sniffs it. "This is a hollow gull bone. Keep it close, and it will help your gift for listening within flow freely."

"Why a gull bone?" wonders Maddie.

"The hollow gull bone is to remind you to quiet your mind and empty yourself of your daily worries and concerns. In other words, the bone reminds you to open to Creator, so you can better tune into the Inner World, where your listening skills come alive."[7]

Maddie sits down at the base of the Oregon white oak and sobs, her legs brushing the ferns. Immediately, Sparks curls up in her lap. Sam, the deer, chipmunk, raccoon, wood duck, dragonflies, and butterflies all sit silently beside her as they and the Mother Tree hold space for both her grief and her joy.

Maddie slowly quiets, and after a few minutes of silence, she says, "What am I gonna do? My family calls me woo-woo. They make fun of me in a mean way. When my Maple died, Mom threatened to send me to a shrink because I was so upset."

"It's hard, I know. Your family can't experience what you do, and for them, it isn't real. It's very sad when you can't share your awareness with your loved ones. However, you have

Sparks who understands and now you have Sam and me, even if I'm just a tree. Nana, Sam's grandmother, will be your ally, too, not to mention all the other plants and trees waiting to meet you. Plus, you have the hollow gull bone!"

"Most people today only believe what they can see and touch and what can be proven by rudimentary science. Most students have a narrow understanding of science, but perhaps you can widen it for them, just a little. Start there. The trees by your school tell me you have a science fair coming up in December. Correct?"

"Yes," Sam and Maddie respond in unison as they exchange stares of amazement.

THE SCIENCE FAIR

Mother Tree says, "It's early October in human time now, so you only have two months to work on your plant experiment because the Science Fair is in early December. The plant kingdom has an experiment to suggest. It will prove human emotions affect the health of plants," Mother Tree says as she outlines the experiment. "Are you willing?"

"Yes!" they agree enthusiastically. The light begins to shimmer, and the form of the Mirror Dragon appears. Maddie's jaw drops, and her eyes widen. "Maybe I *do* need to see a shrink! A silver dragon?!?" Sparks starts barking and then stands at alertness.

"Yes, Maddie, a dragon of mirrors. I would like you to meet SilverLight."

Maddie just stares in amazement for a while, then mutters, "How is this possible?"

"It's complicated! For now, I'll just say dragons are beings of pure-hearted love who exist in a realm our human sense organs normally can't perceive. However, a new breed of human is developing that has the capacity to relate to them. As the English poet Eden Phillpotts said, 'The universe is full of magic things waiting for our senses to grow sharper.'[8] Dragons are not reptiles; they are shape-shifters and take on whatever form is needed in their service to love and joy. Why take the form of a dragon when you can be anything you like? Dragons are the strongest, most versatile life form known to humans, at least in mythology, but they can take any form, so keep your eyes open! They transform oppression into freedom and darkness into light," Mother Tree explains.

"It's a pleasure to meet such a strong, courageous young lady," SilverLight says with a nod.

As Maddie's shock subsides, she begins to feel the sweetness and love coming from SilverLight. She feels at home with her in a way she doesn't with her own family. "Hello SilverLight," she stutters, still adjusting to all that has happened. They all just sit together for a while, two teens surrounded by butterflies, dragonflies, a sentient tree, a deer, chipmunk, raccoon, and wood duck, not to mention a large silver dragon.

As Maddie, Sam, and Sparks walk back to her house, they discuss how to set up the experiment and decide to do it together. SilverLight reminds them that the school has a little-used greenhouse with a few broken windows. As the weather is about to turn chilly, she suggests that they get permission to use it to conduct the experiment, replacing or patching the windows in return. Sam and Maddie do their best to exchange fist bumps with SilverLight, which was awkward at best. Maddie overcomes her shyness, goes to the principal's office during her lunch break and asks who is in charge of access to the old greenhouse. She is given the name of a Ms. Ruby Bradford. "Where is she now?"

The rather busy administrative assistant answers, while still typing on her computer, "Ms. Bradford is at lunch. In the lunchroom."

"Faculty lunchroom or student?" Maddie asks, sounding more like an investigative journalist than a student asking a favor.

"Ms. Bradford is not faculty."

"So she eats with the students? What is she wearing today?"

"A yellow blazer."

"That will be easy to spot. Thank you. I will find her."

Maddie walks to the lunchroom, enters, and scans the room. There are two middle-aged women wearing yellow blazers. One of them looks up at her and says, "Hello."

Maddie lays out her unusual request and Ms. Bradford immediately says, "That is highly unusual, young lady. Furthermore . . ."

SilverLight appears behind Ms. Bradford, glowing with a shimmering bright light, but in an interdimensional way so that only Maddie can see her.

Ms. Bradford continues, "Furthermore, it sounds like an unusually fine idea. I approve it and will secure a key for you. You will have to fill out a log every day showing your entry and exit from the greenhouse. And I want you to give me a tour of your science project when it's done." The two shake hands.

Later in the week, Maddie plants kale, herbs, cabbage, and carrots in her yard, plants that grow year-round in Washington. Then for the sake of the experiment, she selects one plant species to plant in the greenhouse and inside their own houses. She places the seeds in clay pots.

They spend the first week gathering materials: twelve plants: six for school, three for Maddie's house and three for Sam's. They use Sam's dad's light meter to make sure all have the same lighting in each setting. They draw up a feeding and watering schedule that is also consistent for all three locations and they make up twelve signs. Sparks dutifully examines and sniffs all plants and signs.

The first plant in each location has a sign that says: "*Love this plant up,*" and then offers suggestions with additional signs that say, "*You are beautiful. I love you. Thank you for being you. Your leaves are lovely.*"

The second plant's sign reads: "*Abuse this plant. Say mean, nasty things to it.*" They decide no prompts are necessary in this case.

The third sign reads: "*Ignore this plant. Act like it doesn't exist.*" Since there is a greater variety of plants in the greenhouse, there are double the number of plants, and the signs are doubled accordingly.

Maddie is concerned about the plants that will be abused, but when she and Sam are at the garden shop, three plants seem to volunteer to make the sacrifice. Maddie promises to care for them after the experiment. The plants in each location are separated four feet apart, and they have everything ready so that they have the first results by late October. The experiment runs for two months, and they have a presentation with their results ready by early December.

The results are astounding. The plants that are loved, flourish. Those that are emotionally abused are smaller, droopier, and look diseased. The neglected plants are smaller, and their leaves aren't as richly colored, but are otherwise healthy.

It's a snowy day in early December and students are arriving in the school auditorium to set up their displays and results. Maddie only lives a block away, so she pulls her plants and display to the auditorium in a wagon. Sam and Maddie are standing at their booth when the bullies who cornered Maddie at the beginning of school show up.

"Well, if it isn't newbie and woo-woo boy. How are your plants gonna feel when we stomp on them? Will they *s-c-r-e-a-m*? Will you scream when we stomp on you?" they ask menacingly.

Suddenly, ferocious barking fills the auditorium as Sparks races through the crowds and stands protectively in front of Maddie. "Sparks, dogs aren't allowed in here," Maddie whispers, then adds, "but I'm glad you're here."

Sam puts his hand over the crystal in his pocket and he and Maddie whisper, "SilverLight," in unison. A silver flash explodes inside the auditorium, just for a nanosecond, and all motion stops. A nanosecond is a billionth of a second or a very short time.

"We are outside of time now, children. Look beyond their violent, angry expressions. Look deeper. What do you see?"

"I see sad, scared little boys," Maddie says.

"I don't see anything. It's nothingness, a void," Sam responds.

"Yes, they are missing the sweet wine of friendship, and they have filled the void with the intoxicant of power and control over others. Love can't be controlled; it must be free. They hurt and they want others to hurt too. These are the forces that control mass shooters, for example. I will reflect these forces back to them. Watch."

There is another quick, silver flash and motion returns to the auditorium. The bullies' angry faces dissolve into fear, and they quickly back away.

"In that moment, they experienced what their victims experience," SilverLight explains. "Those two bullying students won't come back for more!"

Maddie and Sam exchange expressions of amazement, then their science teacher approaches with the other two judges. It's time for their presentation.

The other judges look dubious as they describe their experiment design and results. "This is a lot more touchy-feely than our usual science experiments, and the results are hard to believe. Plants feeling our emotions? Really?"

Suddenly, Maddie's dad shows up. "Dad, what are you doing here?"

"I couldn't find Sparks, and I followed his footsteps in the snow." Then he turned to the dubious judges. "Maddie is my daughter. She ran her part of the experiment at home. It seemed pretty woo-woo to me, and it took her away from her chores, but I can tell you, she did exactly as she has described, and the plants actually responded, as you see in these charts and diagrams. The results are valid!" That ends the discussion. Sam and Maddie receive an A and a 1st place blue ribbon.

Based on the measurements and the obvious results they were getting, Sam and Maddie formed a hypothesis (an unproven theory) that when we cherish our natural environment and send it gratitude and love, it responds by making our environment more beautiful. In scientific terms, our relationship with nature is "reciprocal"—which means an equal exchange.

Maddie has been going through a lot of growing pains, especially in her heart, but with her success in re-organizing the school greenhouse, and pulling down first place in the Science Fair, her habitual ungroundedness and disconnection from other people is starting to fade. As finals are handed back, Maddie sees that her grades are much better, and knows her father will be even more pleased.

One Saturday afternoon after the Science Fair, Sam and Maddie discuss this hypothesis with Mother Tree, as Sparks and a variety of forest animals stand by their side seeming to listen.

"Your hypothesis is true. The earth's energy runs on reciprocity. Here's another instance: We trees thrive on the CO_2 you exhale, then you breathe the oxygen we provide. We are interdependent. For instance, cloud beings give humans fresh water to drink, but humans, in turn, have the responsibility to keep the springs, rivers, lakes, and oceans clean. In scientific terms, it is called evapotranspiration. Ever see a muddy puddle disappear slowly after the sun comes out? Where does that water go? Well, most of it rises into the sky to become clouds.

Where does the mud go? It returns to the earth to become soil but washed and purified by its dance with the rainwater. After a while, the clouds become so filled with moisture from all the millions of rain puddles evaporating that they start to rain again, and this creates more puddles in an endless cycle."

"But what's the point? If it just goes round and round?" Sam wonders aloud.

"The point is purification! That mud probably has decaying organic matter in it, which can get toxic. The rain cycle is like a round dance between Mother Earth and Father Sky, an exchange of gifts, some might say, but in scientific terms it's a big washing machine that keeps the waters clean and drinkable. The process takes time and washes well, but if humans dirty the water faster than the clouds can keep up, then we have a problem. What happens when the washing machine gets out of balance?"

"It goes bang, bang, bang! I've heard that noise!" answers Sam.

"So it is with the rain cycle. You can't hear the banging, but the amphibians and buds know when something is wrong.

Humans are not fulfilling their role and waters are now polluted. As a result, Mother Earth's energy system is disrupted. We are all experiencing the effects of this imbalance. This brings me to your next assignment, should you choose to accept it."

Sam and Maddie are attentive as Mother Tree continues. "You know the spring that runs through our forest?" They nod in agreement. "Hikers and partiers are littering there. It's contaminating our water supply faster than the rain cycle can handle. When some people throw oil cans and such into a stream it can take thousands of years for the cloud beings and their community of non-human friends to clean it up. Cloud beings have thousands of years, but do you humans? There's probably contaminated runoff from the building and development nearby as well. For now, however, we ask you to put together a cleaning party. Pick up and carry out what you can. Talk to Nana. She will know how to make it a community event. Can we count on you for this?"

Maddie and Sam nod yes. Sparks barks in agreement and SilverLight appears.

THE SWIRLING SPRING

"There's something I want to show you both, if you are up for an adventure," SilverLight says.

Sam and Maddie, sitting at the base of Mother Tree surrounded by animals, look at each other, shrug their shoulders, look at SilverLight, and nod their heads yes.

"Ride along with me as I become a drop of water. Natural waterdrops have lots of microscopic creatures within them, but our drop will be clear and transparent, so you can see. We will start within the water table that feeds the spring. There is fascinating life below the water table, too, but that's another story. I'll just say there are hollows called aquifers in the earth's rock layers that hold water and feed the water table. Ready?"

"Yes," they say together. "Sparks, you and your animal friends stay here and guard Mother Tree," Maddie advises, as they are transported into the waterdrop. The water quickly flows underground.

"It's dark in here!" thinks Sam.

"Welcome to my home, my habitat!" a golden voice says. They turn, and as their eyes slowly adjust to the darkness, they find themselves facing the Western long-toed salamander again. This time she is many times their size, looking terrifyingly dragon-like, her huge powerful claws gripping the muddy soil, her bug eyes shining in the darkness. Maddie screams in surprise, and then covering her mouth says, "Sorry! I didn't mean to scream at you. I guess we're the helpless little creatures now! Sorry to have intruded on your privacy!"

The salamander says, telepathically, "Oh, I wouldn't harm you. I am a messenger of the Mirror Dragon. She is like a Great Aunt to me! And you are her new friends."

"Yes, I am!" SilverLight chuckles. "And Goldie is like my grandniece, and my messenger, as you have heard. I live in big caves, and that is where you'll find my lair, but this is Goldie's lair; she likes tiny caves like this one, under the ground, often near springs. She is very good at looking after herself and her own safety. She is very cautious. You'll be happy to know that her species is in no danger of becoming extinct, at least not here in the Pacific Northwest. But she still needs clean water to swim in."

Goldie says, "I am an amphibian, after all; a creature at home in both land and water." Goldie adds, "If you ever have trouble reaching SilverLight, just talk to a salamander and they will send her the message. Even though I'm a physical being, and she is a purely energetic one, the two realms can overlap. That's why some Native American shamans communicate with the Creator, who is pure, luminous love, through eagles, which are physical." Goldie leaps away—her long tongue whipping out to catch a fly as she jumps.

"There is no light source underground. Look for an opening to the surface," replies Maddie telepathically, as a faint light appears in the distance.

"Yes, we are nearing the spot where the water table meets the earth's surface," responds SilverLight.

"Whoa, it's bumpy!" exclaims Sam as they emerge out of the water table into the spring's swirling current. "These rocks are hard! Let's find a quiet pool." SilverLight guides the waterdrop to a pool protected from the rapid current by tree limbs and stones.

The sun is bright here. As the water in the pool warms, it begins to evaporate, and so the waterdrop rises into the air as vapor. "We're moving up!" exclaims Sam. "It's cooler up here." They continue to rise, and the air continues to cool, "We're surrounded by vapor now, and we're condensing into a bigger and bigger cloud."

"When enough vapor joins us, we will be too heavy to stay in the air and we will fall as rain," explains SilverLight. Indeed, after a while they begin to fall into the soil of the forest as raindrops. Their waterdrop seeps underground. "Wow, we've gone full circle!" exclaims Sam.

When they look out into the underground soil, they are amazed. "This soil is just teeming with life forms! What a busy place! I will never look down on dirt again!" Maddie exclaims in awe.

"Yes, fertile soil is a wondrous sight to behold," agrees SilverLight.

"We're being absorbed by something," Sam notices.

"We're being pulled in by plant root hairs, and soon we will be transported up by the xylem, the plant tissue responsible for distributing water and minerals throughout the plant."

"We're moving up inside some kind of fuzzy green tube," Maddie notices.

"Plants are amazing engineers. Their leaves use energy from the sun to create chemicals for their survival and growth. When the leaves lose water, they create a vacuum pump that draws water up from the roots. They can move water up tall trees, split rocks, and buckle sidewalks," continues Silver-Light.[9]

"We are now moving into a leaf. We will stay here until the guard cells open for us to leave the plant."[10] They wait for nature to take its course. When the guard cells open, the waterdrop evaporates out of the leaf, returning SilverLight, Sam, and Maddie to their own bodies at the foot of Mother Tree.

"Your waterdrop stayed local, but with air currents and various weather patterns, water droplets can travel around the world. All the waters of the world are connected," explains Mother Tree, "as are we all!"

"Indigenous People say 'Water is Life'. Now I see why," ponders Maddie recalling a poster she saw at school. "We sure need to keep the spring clean! Any contaminants in our water affect the health of our soil, air, plants, animals, us, EVERYTHING! Water is Life!" says Mother Tree.

"Let's talk to Nana," Sam agrees.

Nana and Friends of the Spring

Nana's home sits on three acres in the middle of town. She has refused any number of offers to sell for development. Her front yard is filled with a riotous variety of fruit trees all of which are visited during the day by an equally riotous variety of insects: bees, butterflies, dragonflies, and a few spiders too. The fruit is free for anyone's taking, whether human, animal, or insect, and there is still plenty left for Nana to can for winter, as well as for use in her famous jams and cobblers. The backyard is a huge organic garden she and Gramps planted decades ago. Now that Gramps has died and Nana has aged, she has passed the garden over to a community garden co-op. They even have their own seed bank to use. They harvest the seeds from successful plants and save them from year to year. Anyone willing to put in the work gets a key to unlock the gate and free access to the bounty. They donate a lot to the local food bank too. As Sam, Maddie, and Sparks enter Nana's house, a group of people are leaving. Nana's large open living room has chairs arranged in a circle.

"Hello, Sam! And who is with you?" Nana calls out.

"Nana, meet my friend Maddie and her dog Sparks."

"Oh sure, you did the science fair thing together," she says as she reaches down to pet Sparks. Sparks looks up at her with adoring eyes. "I am still remembering to praise my plants and trees, and you see how they are responding! I've never seen them so lush and happy! I have cookies in the kitchen left from our community meeting. Would you like a dog biscuit, Sparks?" Sparks barks excitedly, and they all laugh. "That's a yes!" Maddie agrees. "Milk or lemonade?" asks Nana. They both choose lemonade as they go into the kitchen.

"Nana, we've been spending time in the forest," begins Sam. Nana returns her knowing smile but says nothing. "People are littering all around the spring. We're worried about contamination. So much life depends on this spring, including our famous long-toed salamanders who swim in this water! It's gonna take a community effort to clean it and keep it clean. Can you help us?"

Nana reflects for a moment. "I love Ambystoma macrodactylum! I'm in. Let's brainstorm. What do we need to accomplish this?"

"We need a group of people, biodegradable garbage bags, and a large dumpster," suggests Sam.

"How will we prevent littering there in the future?" wonders Maddie. "While working on my science project, I read about Dr. Zion's research at Marist College that many people are more motivated by songs about combating pollution and climate change than hard data."[11] [12]

Nana responds, "I saw a concert by Pete Seeger back in 1967 singing a love song to 'My Dirty Stream' and it did more to make me a Planet Activist Defender Protector than all the books I've ever read. Music touches our hearts. I'll sing it for you."

Sailing down my dirty stream
Still I love it and I'll keep the dream
That some day, though maybe not this year
My Hudson River, will once again run clear[13]

"Well, that *does* motivate me! What about a sign with eco-friendly litter bags like they do for dogs? This will all cost money," Maddie continues.

Nana stands up, raises her hands above her head and proclaims, "Friends of the Spring!" Sam smiles and is waiting for her to start dancing as she often does. "We have lots of groundwork to do," Nana continues. "I will present the idea to the groups that meet here. The community garden co-op and the hiking group both might be interested in helping. We'll see."

"I'm in the school newspaper club. I'll write an article. Also, Sparks and I are working on getting our therapy dog certificate. The others in the class might be interested as well," Maddie offers.

"I heard there is a study group forming after school to explore climate change and environmental issues. I'll check that out," adds Sam. "We can always count on Mom and Dad." He notices Maddie lower her head sadly. Nana notices, too, and gives her a hug.

"The soccer field and forest are part of a county park. We would have to notify the county commissioners of any major plans, and that could be a problem. Good old politics! However, there is a lot we can do as small groups visiting the park. But right now the sun's setting, you two. Best you get home before dark. Come back when you want to talk again," Nana says as she gives them bags of cookies and guides them out the door.

They each talk to anyone who will listen about cleaning the spring. Nana describes the project to the community groups using her home. Maddie writes a column in the school newspaper, and the English teacher who advises the newspaper becomes enthusiastic. Sam discusses the issue in his afterschool club on climate change, and the biology teacher advising the club gets motivated as well. The two teachers talk to the principal and, as a result, the school makes the proposed clean-up a school-wide event. The art department makes posters and flyers; many of the teachers design units studying the proposed clean-up. For instance, the math classes work out the capacity of the dumpster, how much garbage can fit in it, and how many biodegradable trash bags are needed. They also calculate the cost of the project. The biology classes study the water cycle. The English classes post an essay contest on the subject: *Why Cleaning the Spring is Important and What I Will Do to Help.*

Nana begins the process of setting up a nonprofit organization called "Friends of the Spring," which will make tax-deductible donations possible in the future. It can take up to a year, so in the meantime, they set up a booth at the local farmer's market where Nana sells her produce and famous cookies. The children create a colorful donation box labeled *Contribute to a Cleaner Spring.* They have flyers available on the table, and when customers ask about it, the children take the opportunity to explain.

Sam contacts a student vocal group through school and asks if they know any Pete Seeger songs and they say, "Yes." When Sam asks if they know *My Dirty Stream*, they start singing it. Sam says, "You wanna sing that song at the next Farmer's Market?"

"Yes, sure, and we can sing it at our next concert, and you can hand out flyers," the choral director responds.

They publicize it at school and in the groups that meet at Nana's. When they have enough money for renting the dumpster, a sign, and biodegradable litter bags, Nana arranges for the three of them to attend a county commissioners' meeting.

Sam and Maddie spend long hours on the phone, talking and planning. They talk about a lot more than the spring. Maddie describes the town and school she left. They chat about their favorite sports, and Sam shares his dream of being soccer captain. Best of all, they share funny stories and laugh—deep belly laughs that take their breath away. Sam has a cell phone, but Maddie doesn't, and her rambling marathon talks with Sam start tying up her parents' land line and it doesn't go over well.

THE COMMISSIONERS' MEETING

The night of the meeting, Nana and Sam drive to Maddie's home to pick her up. When she comes out of the house, Nana and Sam look at each other, concerned. Maddie's eyes are red and puffy, and her blouse is buttoned in a cockeyed manner. She looks disheveled and miserable.

"Please go to the back seat, Sam, so she can sit next to me," Nana says.

"Maddie, what's wrong? Are you okay?" Nana askes softly as Sam goes to the back and Maddie to the front passenger seat.

Maddie starts sobbing. She tries to talk, but her sobs make her hard to understand. "Dad . . . dishes . . . phone . . . scared!"

Nana takes Maddie's hand and waits for her to calm and Sam feels the crystal warm in his pocket. Suddenly, the car is filled with a cool, soft, comforting mist. Maddie calms, but only Sam recognizes SilverLight's healing presence. When Maddie is ready to talk, they learn she's been so engrossed in the spring clean-up project that she's been neglecting her chores. She's been tying up their land line talking to Sam, and her father is fed up. He's threatening to ground her.

"I've never seen him so angry. It was scary! Sparks felt my dad's anger also and stood between us and growled. Why didn't he just ask me to get off the phone instead of exploding?" she wonders.

"Your father must be under a lot of pressure, Maddie. I'm so sorry sweetie," Nana says soothingly.

"Yes, Mom says he is being mistreated at work, but why is he taking it out on me?" Maddie sobs.

"Hurt people hurt people, Maddie, but we can help break the cycle," Nana says quietly. "Tomorrow is Saturday. We will take you to the forest for healing. Did you know in Japan doctors prescribe 'forest bathing' as a medicine for anxiety and depression? Nature heals."

"What's forest bathing?" Maddie mumbles in confusion.

Nana responds: "Sitting in nature is restorative. It's an antidote to the constant stimulation and stressors of modern life. Studies have shown being in a forest environment reduces the amount of cortisol in our bodies—a stress-related hormone, while also decreasing our pulse rate and blood pressure. It also relaxes our nervous systems."[14]

Maddie's hand automatically finds the hollow gull bone she keeps in her jacket pocket, and she feels Maple's love. "Yes, late morning please, so I can make sure I have completed all my chores."

Nana helps Maddie rebutton her blouse, gives her a drink of water and a tissue to wipe her face. When she is soothed, they drive on to the commissioners' board meeting.

The commissioners are seated in a semi-circle around a large table. Nana guides the children to three folding chairs near the front of the room. Sam and Maddie are the only children present and feel a bit nervous. Maddie shoots Sam a look that says, "It's all so official and boring!" The agenda is lengthy, and it takes forever for the spring issue to be addressed. When the topic is finally introduced, the commissioners are restless and skeptical. Nana has the children pass out photos of the litter and pollution in and around the spring while she explains their proposed plan.

"Hey, what's a little beer in our spring water?" a big burly commissioner sneers as he looks at the photo of a beer can in the water while the others laugh. Maddie and Sam look at each other nervously.

Nana says, "It's not just our spring water, Sir!"

The burly man says, "Yes it is. It's in our township!"

Nana responds quietly, "That's not what I meant."

Maddie fears a conflict about to erupt and feels her gull bone warming, and when she puts her hand in her pocket to grasp it, she hears Mother Tree say, "Look in the eyes of the woman on the right side of the table. She understands. Hold her gaze." And Maddie does.

Nana backs off from waxing poetically about the Western long-toed salamander, but smiles and pulls a recent study entitled *The Far-reaching Effects of Pollution in our Local Springwater* out of her bag and cheerfully says, "This study from our local university's Department of Ecology should answer this question." She opens the top copy in the stack to a color photo of a beautiful long-toed salamander, displaying her fabulous golden-yellow racing stripe, and holds the picture up for all to see, then hands out the copies.

The woman commissioner on the right speaks up, "I don't know nothin' about no big nose salamander, but we've been having trouble with contaminants in our drinking water at home, and it has been traced back to something called pollution runoff. I'm in favor of this project." The other commissioners never seem to fully grasp the importance of the proposal but are swayed enough by their colleague to finally agree to it. "After all," Nana says soothingly, "It won't cost the county any money." They do want to know what the sign will say and *Bring Out What You Take In! Keep Our Spring Clean!* is agreed upon. The woman commissioner offers to make sure the sign is ready. Nana seems amused by it all, but Maddie and Sam are relieved and exhausted by the time they leave.

TOGETHERNESS

The next day, Nana and Sam pick up Maddie and Sparks at noon. Nana has prepared a picnic lunch of hard-boiled eggs collected from her hens and fruits and vegetables harvested from her garden. She made her delicious hummus dip too, along with a thermos of homemade lemonade. For Sparks, she has brought eggs, cheese, and baby carrots. They put a blanket down at the foot of Mother Tree and feast. A murder of crows perch on Mother Tree's branches and Nana offers them seeds from her pockets. "I've noticed animals show up around you and Sparks, Maddie," Nana says. Maddie smiles as she takes another bite of her peach.

"Nana, I'd love to hear about your travels. Is this a good time?" Sam asks.

"Well, I grew up in Indiana. I remember standing in a cornfield my junior year in high school thinking, 'I want to go to a place as different from Indiana as possible.' After college I traveled a lot, mostly in Africa and South America. I taught English as a second language to support myself.

"I went to Africa first and lived in a compound with four Bantu families. We each had a small concrete home, cooked over a fire, and drew water from a well. The women had to teach me how to draw water without fraying the rope. They thought my ignorance was funny and said they didn't know a white person could live without air conditioning.

"I was most impressed with their communal spirit. For instance, when a woman in our compound wanted a divorce, both extended families came together with a presiding chief.

The woman told her side of the story and her family spoke to support her position. Then the man and his family told his side of the story. The whole community was present. In the end, she was able to return to her birth family with her child and some belongings. Everyone heard both sides of the conflict and had an opportunity to speak. This was so different from how I grew up in Indiana, where each family lives privately in their own home, decisions are made based on the needs of the individual, and conflicts are handled by a lawyer. Our Western culture isolates families in so many ways. We humans are social animals and need the connection of community. This is why your grandfather and I supported community efforts and why I've turned my home into a community center. We are facing many forces beyond our control, and we need to work together to find life-supporting solutions. Indigenous cultures say we need to make community decisions based on what is good for seven future generations.

"Traditional African tribes believe nature is sentient. In other words, capable of feeling, feeling and perceiving things and for the first time in my life, I could feel this too. For instance, there is a river called Bondoukou, and I could feel its powerful spirit. I never felt anything like this before or after. I learned that while humans all need the same basic things—love, food, and shelter, our experiences on earth differ, depending on the stories that guide our cultural beliefs."

"What about South America, Nana?" Sam asks.

"Later, Sam. Maddie needs the forest today."

After eating, Maddie's hand automatically finds her hollow gull bone and she feels like taking a walk. "May Maple's love guide my steps," she thinks to herself as she stands up with Sparks by her side. "We're going to explore," she tells the others.

Spring sunlight is filtering through the tree, so everything sparkles. She hears a symphony of bird songs and sees a rustling in the branches. Her steps sink softly into the leaves and mosses covering her path. She sees movement in the bushes and catches glimpses of small animals. She feels exquisitely alive. After walking for a while, she is guided to a large Douglas fir tree and sits down with her back to it. Sparks sits at her feet. Maddie hears an elderly voice speaking but can't tell where it is coming from, then realizes it's coming from behind her.

"We Douglas firs are a protector species. We offer protection to small plants and animals, and we can also help you. When you feel unsafe, go to the Douglas fir in the greenbelt behind your house and sit like this to release your fear. This is the tree Maple has chosen for you."

"Am I really hearing you talk?" Maddie asks.

"Yes, my tree nature is speaking to your human nature. All nature is sentient, capable of feeling and perceiving, but in many different ways which humans can scarcely imagine. Did you know even slime mold can make decisions?[15] This is why when Native Americans bless, 'All My Relations', they mean all life forms. We are all a part of nature, and we are all connected on this beautiful earth."

Suddenly, a small squirrel approaches Maddie and sits down right in front of her. It has a brownish-gray back, tawny-orange belly, and a white eye-ring.[16] Maddie recognizes it as a Douglas squirrel.

"Hello," Maddie hears telepathically, "I'm Douglas Squirrel at your service. I'm here to remind you to be playful, even when planning for a long winter. You have all the resources you need for your life within you. Listen to and follow the path Creator has chosen for you and what you need will come. Just don't forget to sing and dance along the way. And try to stay in balance!"

Maddie suddenly feels wonderful. "Thank you, Douglas Fir Tree. Thank you, Douglas Squirrel," she says as she and Sparks get up and she skips back to Nana and Sam. They sip lemonade and talk late into the afternoon.

CELEBRATION

Much time has passed, and now it's a sunny Saturday in June. There is one more week of school. Sam's junior varsity soccer team has just played its last game of the season, a playoff game which they lost. As a first-year player, and an eighth grader, Sam is in junior varsity, but next year he will be 15 and in the senior varsity of his middle school and facing more pressure. During that playoff game, SilverLight worked closely with Sam, showing him how to be more assertive and less fearful, and how to mirror everything happening on the field. He begins to feel where all his teammates are on the field—even if he can't see them.

All the major exams are over and the end-of-school dance is the only big event left on the school calendar. The spring is cleared, and the dumpster is filled and waiting to be removed.

The sign is put at the entrance of the forest. Dumpsters aren't usually picked up on Saturdays, but one of Sam's classmates won the art department's poster contest. His father works for the Sanitation Department and arranges to pick up the dumpster with a recycling truck decorated with posters from the contest. A huge cheer erupts from the crowd as it is hauled away. Maddie's therapy dog class is present and the owners and therapy dogs disperse amongst the crowd offering licks and cuddles to all. There is also food, music, and dancing. Nana leads everyone in the dance—everyone except Maddie—that is. Maddie doesn't dance, and Nana dances the most.

As the crowd is dispersing, Sam gets up his courage, "Maddie, do you wanna go to the end-of-school dance with me?"

Maddie blushes and shuffles her feet awkwardly, "I dunno, Sam. I dunno how to dance. I'd just step on your feet. And I can't remember the last time I wore a dress."

Sam takes a deep breath and silently asks, "SilverLight give me the right words." Then he continues, "There isn't a dress code, although most students do dress up. We don't have to dance. Nana and Mom are helping with refreshments. We can just sit in a corner and eat Nana's cookies and drink Mom's lemonade. Maddie, we've shared so much. No one else would understand."

"Is it a date?" she asks.

"If you want it to be."

"Not yet, Sam. So many worlds are opening up for us. Adding dating would just be too much for me right now."

"Okay, we will go as friends."

"Deal," Maddie agrees, and they awkwardly shake hands.

The night of the dance, they help Nana and Sarah with the refreshments and find a quiet corner to eat and talk. "I'm glad you invited me," Maddie says as they drop her off back home. "I guess for kids who see dragons, nothing's impossible, but dancing is gonna take me some time."

One afternoon, a few weeks after school is out, Maddie and Sam are playing fetch with Sparks in the field when they notice some boys with spray cans around the sign. Sparks starts to growl. "Are those the bullies that bothered us at the science fair, Maddie?"

She nods yes, looking concerned. "What do we do?"

Sam unzips his jacket pocket and takes out his crystal. He holds it in his palm and says SilverLight's name. He and Maddie see her faint outline glittering near the sign. She blows silver smoke towards the bullies. Startled, they freeze, then flee. Maddie and Sam see their terrified faces as they run past. "What did you do?" they ask in unison, as Sparks lets down his guard.

"They are troubled, filled with aggression and rage. I sent them a mirror and they saw themselves again. You know these boys?"

The young people nod their heads yes. SilverLight responds, "Tell Nana what you saw. It is against the law to deface county property. She will notify the authorities. The shock has torn a hole in the boys' defenses. They will be given an opportunity to change. Whether they choose to accept it or not is up to them."

When they talk to Nana, she says *Friends of the Spring* has enough money to repaint the sign. "Can you have sign makers create a picture of a silver dragon with the words, '*Litter at your own risk*'?" quips Sam. Nana chuckles and stares at them for a few moments and then says, "I'll see." The county commissioners approve the plan, and the sign is never again defaced.

THE BREAK-IN

A week later, Sam walks into the kitchen and sees his distraught mother on the phone. He hears Nana screaming on the other end. Worried, he moves close enough to hear. "They broke in the front door. The front room is trashed. I was afraid to go through the house or check the garden alone. I'm waiting for the police in my car."

"We'll be right there, Mom. Lock your doors and press the panic button on your key fob if necessary."

"Sam, call Dad. Let's go." They race to the car and Mom drives while Sam explains to Dad. They arrive and find the police helping Nana out of her car. Strong, invincible Nana is shaking. While the police go through the house and garden, Mom, Sam, and Dad surround Nana and hold her until the police return.

"The way is clear, but the house is a mess. Looks like they escaped through the back alley. If you are ready, go through the house and make a list of what's missing, but don't move anything until our forensic photographer is done. How did they do this unnoticed?" the policeman wonders aloud.

"Nana's home is a community center. People are coming and going all the time, and the fruit trees in the front yard block the view of the doors and windows," answers Sarah, as they all walk into the house.

The furniture is overturned, and every shelf and drawer has been opened and emptied. "Guess they were looking for money or jewels. None here," Nana thinks aloud. She is stoic until she sees the seed bank strewn on the wooden floor. She sits down on the floor and sobs. "The future," she moans in between sobs.

"Mom, we can sort out these seeds together when the police are done. I doubt they came to steal seeds. When you are ready, let's find out what they *did* steal. I'll be right by your side. Let me know if you need some time." Nana nods her head, and Sam's dad helps her up.

The only things missing from inside are the cookies Nana had made this morning. In the backyard, the tool shed is empty. Tools and equipment gathered over a half-century—gone. The padlock on the back gate is badly broken. "Guess they used our bolt cutter," sighs Nana. "I do have an inventory I made for insurance purposes."

Sam feels the crystal warming in his pocket. He takes it out and hears SilverLight say, "Give her the crystal. She can call me when she needs protection. You don't need it anymore. We are merged. When you need me, just call my name and I will call yours."

Later, when the police are talking to Sarah and Frank, Sam talks to Nana alone. He puts the crystal in Nana's palm, and a soft comforting mist envelopes them both. SilverLight's image appears. "Ahh, I see. What is this dragon's name?"

"SilverLight," Sam responds.

"SilverLight is a healer dragon, isn't she? I feel my shock and fear fading away. I've always wanted a dragon partner," Nana whispers softly.

"This can be arranged," says SilverLight telepathically to them both.

Crystal in hand, Nana throws her arms around Sam and for a moment time stops; the air sparkles, and they are filled with a Mirror Dragon's pure-hearted love.

"I will put this in the medicine pouch my friend Phillip gave me. He's one of the 4000 Puyallup Native Americans still living in this area. The Puyallup are cedar people. Their long houses and canoes were traditionally made from cedar, for instance. Papa and I consulted Phillip before planting our cedar trees here. We jokingly call him Chief Calming Thunder because of his ability to resolve community conflicts. The Indigenous People still remember how to live sustainably on this land. We have much to learn from them."

"What's a medicine pouch?" Sam asks.

"It's a sacred container created and used by Indigenous Peoples. They put sacred objects that contain protection and healing in it. I wear it around my neck, close to my heart. It's a great honor to receive this as a gift."

There is a write-up in the local paper about the break-in. The article describes Nana's role in the community resulting in an outpouring of support. In a short time, community fundraising replaces what insurance doesn't, including a monitored alarm system. The community reciprocates for all her contributions to its well-being. Nana is deeply grateful, most of all, for Sam and SilverLight.

Facing a Changing Earth

Summer begins, and several months pass without conflicts with the sign bullies. Sam continues to master his footwork while speaking to SilverLight every day. He prepares for playing as a senior on his middle school's varsity team. He is now 15 and entering 9th grade, as is Maddie. Sam and Maddie are helping Nana in her garden while Sparks rests under a shade tree. Sam's mother likes to use worm castings manure for her kitchen garden, and Nana has a worm farm.

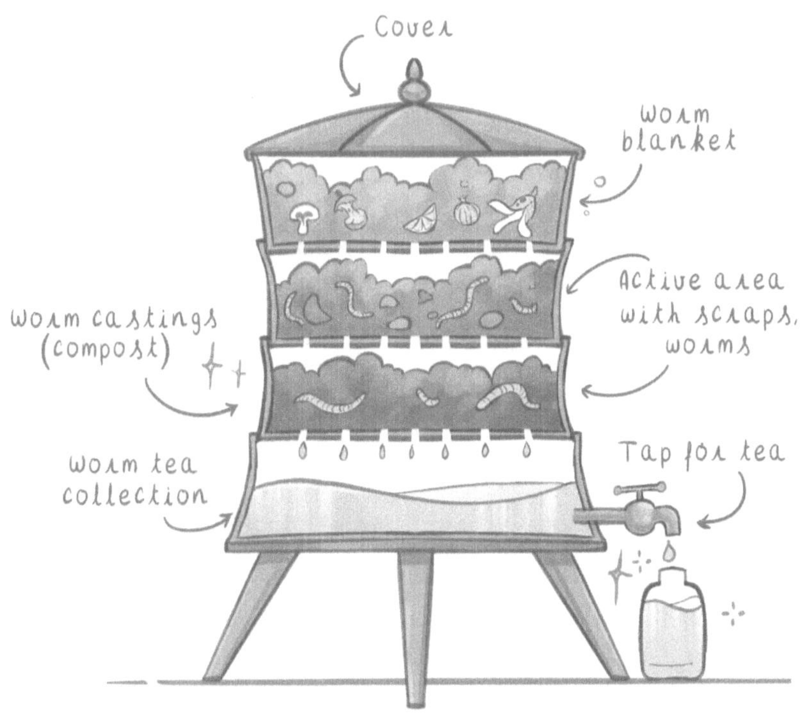

WORM FARM

"We can feed the worms when we gather the worm castings manure," Nana explains. "We put the food on one level and gather the worms' manure from the one below. Worms like fruit and veggie scraps, eggshells, bread, cheese, coffee grounds, tea bags, any cooked vegetarian scraps, but NO meat, fish, or manures. The worms can access smaller pieces faster, so no dense garden waste. Nana shows them how to lift the straw covering of the worm farm, where to place the food scraps, and how to gather the castings manure.[17]

As they work, they notice smoke in the air. "In the Pacific Northwest, our air is usually clean and fresh, but the fires in the south and east are bringing us smoke," comments Nana.

"So many fires, hurricanes, tornadoes, floods, and earthquakes, Nana. Will there be an earth for us when we grow up?" wonders Sam.

"It's scary," adds Maddie. "I have nightmares about dying trees!"

"In Eastern Washington, our friend's farm burned to the ground—the house, barn, and surrounding grasslands. So sad!" sighs Sam. "Do you think it could happen here?"

"Not without a fight, Sam," Nana answers. "There was a big fire four years ago, and we held several round table discussions and came up with some emergency strategies that are now in place. We knew that climate change was just going to keep making matters worse and causing more wildfires on a larger scale, so we organized a network of volunteers to help the local fire departments do their jobs—to help them help us.

"We located several unmanned fire towers and assigned volunteers to do 'fire watch duty' whenever the Smoky Bear fire hazard signs were in the red. Two people would sit on the fire towers and phone in with walkie-talkies at signs of smoke or flame above the forest canopy. Others volunteered to do fire watch from mountaintops during fire hazard times and also from top floors of high buildings. This has been very effective."

Maddie says, "Gee, must get boring up there!"

"You bring a book, Maddie," quips Sam.

"I'd do crossword and Sudoku puzzles," Maddie laughs.

Nana continues, "Spotting a fire is not enough. You have to be able to put it out. With all the water shortages, this has become an issue. Now each town has dug a pond at a low place or wetland with road access where a pump truck can load up enough water to fight a big fire or two."

Sam says, "That's a cool idea. What else did they decide?"

Nana says, "They trained volunteers how to build fire roads and fire breaks, manage backfires and dig trenches. They also taught them how to use a Polaski and other firefighting tools. We also hold many first-aid classes and encourage every family to store enough first-aid kits to help themselves and at least one neighbor."

"Are we what they call a prepper?" Sam asks.

Nana answers, "Being prepared for a likely emergency is common sense. Trying to prepare for World War III may or may not be a good idea for your average citizens. We've learned to be self-sufficient here. Some people might call us preppers, but we know this land. This is why community is so important. Isolated individuals cannot handle what we are facing now. We must work together to survive."

The conversation turns to all that is being lost, and a sadness fills their hearts. Nana reminds them of the Great Fire of 1910 that reached the northeastern corner of Washington State and threatened Spokane. She says, "Millions of acres of forest were destroyed and many lives lost, but it sure got the forest service's attention. At first, they became overprotective of trees and caused other problems, but over the years, they learned the importance of controlled burning and letting some fires happen naturally, while developing various techniques of fire management, some of them quite familiar to Native Americans. Our trees are precious to us, but we must learn to let them live and die in balance with the four elements and this includes fire. Foresters need to take out some debris that can become fuel for forest fires, a process natives call 'Combing the Mother's Hair.' If we never comb our hair, it becomes tangled! The same with the forests. If we untangle them in the right way, we can increase the amount of sunlight, air, and water that reaches the center of the forest, encouraging growth and reducing the threat of fire. We as humans can also create 'edges,' sunny areas at the outer perimeter of a forest that bear fruit and nuts and attract animals. You see, humans can be good stewards and help the wild processes of nature but only by walking in balance with all life forms."

Suddenly Nana feels warmth coming from the crystal in her medicine pouch. She takes it out, holds it in her palm, and feels SilverLight say, "Come to the Oregon white oak tree in the forest by the soccer field."

At the same time, Sam and Maddie hear SilverLight say telepathically, "Come to the Mother Tree."

Nana, Sam, Maddie, and Sparks look at each other, astonished! Without a word, they all get in Nana's car, deliver the castings to Sam's mother, and drive to the soccer field. Within half an hour, all four are standing at the foot of the Mother Tree.

"As you know," starts SilverLight telepathically, "much of the earth is being destroyed. We have lost a billion acres of trees worldwide and the rate of deforestation is escalating quickly. Let me show you."[18] With their inner eyes, Sam, Maddie, and Nana see trees cleared for agriculture, felled by logging operations and cut down for urban development. Sam thinks of Mother Tree, and a tear falls down his cheek.

"I recently read in National Geographic that 80% of earth's land animals and plants live in forests," added Nana.

"Yes," continues SilverLight, "fewer trees result in less protection from the sun and higher temperatures. Higher temperatures affect all the two-leggeds, plants, and animals who live in the forest. Trees store carbon and they release this carbon when felled.[19] We've lost 60% of Mother Earth's animals since 1970."

"Oh no," cries Maddie as she thinks of losing Douglas Squirrel.

"I read that 40% of plant species are at risk as well," laments Nana.[20] "We are destroying the very web of life that nourishes and protects us." They are all quiet for a while as the vision of a destroyed world under siege fills their inner eyes.

"However," SilverLight continues, "Mother Earth is not dying. She has been through worse, and She has a plan, a plan of rejuvenation. Her plan is being created in the Inner World now and, little by little, as more humans join the effort, Her plan will emerge into the Outer World. It's already happening.

Organic farmers, for instance, are rotating crops, using natural methods for pest control, and fertilizing the soil."

"Who are these humans, SilverLight?" asks Nana.

GALACTIC GUARDIANS

"You are! We call you the Galactic Guardians. You still have to finish school, so a committed study of natural science and how we can better serve the earth will have to wait, but we will find mentors to teach you what is appropriate for your situation at this time. Galactic Guardians come from every land, race, and age. Your mission, should you choose to accept it, is to support the new world being created, even as the old world is destroyed.

"As Galactic Guardians you might be inspired by learning of the Rainbow Warrior Prophecy, a Hopi prophecy which tells us that when the earth is ravaged and animals are dying, a new generation of people shall appear from many colors, classes, and creeds and who by their actions and deeds shall make the earth green again. They will be known as the Warriors of the Rainbow. As the late Thomas Banyacya, spokesman of the Hopi Traditional Elders states, 'As Native Americans, we believe the Rainbow is a sign from the Spirit of all things. It is a sign of the union of all people, like one big family. The unity of all humanity, many tribes, and peoples, is essential.'[21] Galactic Guardians should have a special respect for the insights of Native Americans and all Indigenous People, whose ancestral teachings are what guide Galactic Guardians along their path in service to Mother Earth."

With raised eyebrows and widened eyes, Sam and Maddie stand slack-jawed. Nana, on the other hand, doesn't seem surprised one bit, just intrigued and fully engaged. "Yes, we are Galactic Guardians," she whispers softly, "and I will contact Phillip, our 'Chief Calming Thunder' and ask how I can learn more about working in harmony with Indigenous Peoples."

THE NEW WORLD

"Creator loves us and created Mother Earth from this love," SilverLight explains. "Love is the Great Connector. Many humans have forgotten this truth. When people live in their minds, judging, criticizing, and fearing those who think differently, they separate themselves. They become isolated and disconnected, lost in their thoughts. They can even become physically ill.

"Mother Earth, on the other hand, thrives on reciprocity. For instance, we are nourished by plants. If we honor the nature of each plant, giving it what it needs to grow, then it is healthy. When we eat it, we are healthy too. Everything organically created on this beautiful planet has a nature, a purpose, and requires a certain soil to flourish. We are all interconnected so when we harm the soil, air, and water needed by others, we harm ourselves as well. Our bodies are like little planets. How we think about the earth planet affects how we think about our bodies—what we put into our bodies as food reflects our attitudes towards the earth, and the earth can get sick just as we can," SilverLight continues.

"Humans receive many gifts from Mother Earth, and in return you are responsible for caring for Her, keeping Her waters clean and Her soils rich. This beautiful world is based on reciprocity and love.

"There is a deep wisdom within Mother Earth. She knows what is needed to bring human beings back into natural balance with their bodies and with all of life. She needs humans who understand what has gone awry and are willing to work towards correcting the imbalance. Are you willing?"

"Willing to do what?" asks Maddie, with a tinge of worry in her voice.

"The new world, balanced in love, is being created in the Inner Realm. In time, it will manifest in the outer. The first step is for you to travel within and see it for yourselves. Are you ready for an adventure?" asks SilverLight.

"How do we travel within?" asks Maddie. "Do you have a Magic Schoolbus?"

"We have my tail, actually. But most of the time we travel within by maintaining a state of gratitude and innocence," continues SilverLight, "by quieting our minds and opening our hearts to unconditional love. Observe your thoughts. Is your mind full of fears, worries, and things you must do? These thoughts take us away from the present moment. When we are fully present there is more room in us for love. You will find your own way of quieting. Some go 'forest bathing' or soak in water. Others run or ride a bicycle until their minds clear. Singing or getting lost in music helps too. Experiment and see what works for you. If you can't still your mind, try just focusing on one thought or sound or word for a while—or one object in nature. This works pretty well."

"Sparks loves unconditionally!" exclaims Maddie.

"Yes, Sparks doesn't love you for how you look, how clever you are, or what you own. He loves you just the way you are! Being with animals can quiet our minds too."

"And treats! He loves when I give him treats!" continues Maddie.

"Of course, you provide what he needs to grow into his true nature, and he gives you love," continues SilverLight.

"Show us how to travel within, SilverLight," whispers Nana.

"I will. I am going to shape-shift into a sailboat named Song of Innocence. I sing my Song of Innocence by feeling my love for my dragon eggs in the hatchery."

"DRAGON EGGS!" shriek Sam, Maddie, and Nana all at once.

"Where are your eggs?" shouts Maddie.

"Where is your home and your family?" Nana asks simultaneously.

"What promises did YOU make to Creator, SilverLight?" Sam wonders, adding to the chorus.

"Aren't you all full of questions today!" chuckles Silver-Light. "My soul family lives in the far reaches of the universe, light-years away from here. We don't need our earth bodies at home. We have light bodies of pure energy, know each other by our energetic signatures, and travel with the speed of thought. We have missions all over the multiverse. Yours is not the only universe, you know. There are many others. We are shape-shifters and take on whatever shape is needed for each mission. We are amazingly flexible, and our minds are open to every possibility. We are always seeking knowledge, but never at the cost of pure knowing—never at the cost of innocence. Those of us who have chosen to support Mother Earth at this time have an outpost in the Realm of Possibilities. That's where my eggs are! We will be sailing into the Realm of Possibilities today, but not to my family's outpost. I will take you there another time, I promise, Sam. Now back to today's agenda. I sing a Song of Gratitude and Love for my eggs." A gentle tone fills the air creating a feeling of pure innocence.

"You must sing your own Songs of Gratitude and Innocence to come on board," explains SilverLight.

"I sing a Song of Gratitude and Love for my dog, Sparks," sings Maddie, as she and Sparks board the sailboat.

"I sing how grateful I felt when Sam gave me the crystal," sings Nana.

"I sing in gratitude remembering the moment Mother Tree first spoke to me," sings Sam.

As their Songs of Innocence and Gratitude harmonize, they fuel the sailboat as it rises out of the forest and travels upon invisible waves into the inner Realm of Possibilities.

They share the sensation of flying upwards, and the higher they go, the more light surrounds them and the lighter they feel. A welcoming mist envelopes them.

"Where are we?" asks Nana.

"We are in the Realm of Possibilities. Past, present, and future possibilities all exist at once here. Our perception of time, as they say, is what keeps everything from happening at once. That being said, we are going to visit a future possibility, one which might affect our present circumstances in unexpected ways. As you will see, many souls are working to bring this possibility into reality." SilverLight falls silent for a few moments, and no one on the sailboat wishes to break this silence, so full of reverberations.

"Who gave you the name SilverLight?" asks Maddie as they sail along.

"I was hatched in our home world, light-years from earth. Our home world is out of time. We are eternal beings, just as you are. I remember first seeing my parents' sparkling energy and feeling their unconditional love. I was named Silver-Light because of my silver scales. Dragons only need about six months in your earthly time to grow from hatchling to adult, but it is a precious time for everyone. It is a time of playfulness and joy, as we develop our skills and discover our gifts.

"We discovered my scales are reflectors, and I possessed the gifts of a Mirror Dragon. Mirror Dragons reflect both the light and the shadow sides of existence; thus, I was given the name SilverLight. The other hatchlings could see their gifts more clearly when reflected back from me. On the other hand, dragons who had been wounded were brought back to our home world for healing, and in my company, they could see their wounds more clearly, too, a first step in healing.

"When we are full grown, we specialize. My family has served Mother Earth since Her creation. We remember a time when humans and dragons co-created life on earth together. The forces that feed on judgment, violence, hatred, and greed have taken earth's inhabitants down a very dark road and are creating chaos on earth at this time. However, their time is ending. There is a new world dawning on earth for those willing to face their wounds of heart and spirit and choose healing and love. As a Mirror Dragon, I reflect back to you your future transformational abilities as a species."

Slowly the mist dissolves along with the sailboat and SilverLight, Nana, Sam, Maddie, and Sparks find themselves in a luscious flower garden. The ground is covered in tiny flowers, some white star-shaped and others blue-bell shaped.

"Let's take a walk," guides SilverLight.

As they walk on the flowered ground cover, a scent is released. "I would call this scent Joy," says Maddie, and they all beamingly agree. "Listen," Maddie continues. The sound of quiet bells fills the air.

"Every created being has its own song. This is the Song of Creation for these flowers," whispers SilverLight. "Each note provides the exact energy needed for them to flourish."

"Oh, thank you for bringing us here, SilverLight," says Sam.

"Quiet joy, quiet joy," whispers Nana.

Maddie spontaneously starts singing,

> "Beautiful flowers white and blue,
> Filling our steps with quiet joy
> We walk and sing together with you."

As Maddie sings and Sparks wags his tail, the scents and sounds amplify. SilverLight, Nana, and Sam join in, and for a time, they are lost in the wonder of it all.

As they walk, the landscape begins to change. "I hear running water," Maddie notices.

"Ahhh, the River of Hope. Let's follow the sound," suggests SilverLight as she guides them further.

After a while, they come to a riverbank. Beside it is a trellis made from a living tree. The trellis is covered with white stars and bluebells; inside the trellis stand two beings. One is as tall as Nana and has the shape of a tall bluebell, and the other appears as a glowing white star. When Bluebell bows, quiet bells fill the air. When Whitestar pulses, scents of joy spread far and wide.

"Greetings Bluebell and Whitestar," SilverLight calls out as she steps forward in a playful dragon dance. "I would like you to meet Nana, Sam, Maddie, and Sparks, our new apprentices," SilverLight points to the three humans and their canine friend respectfully, with a grand sweep of her tail.

"Greetings," responds Bluebell telepathically, and as he bows, the air is filled with bell chimes once again.

"You are welcome here," Whitestar sings telepathically as she pulses joyful scents into the air.

"I need to sit down," says Nana wiping her brow. "This is a bit much to take in. I need to rest."

"Ah, rest and rejuvenation are our specialties," Whitestar replies. "Beloved Trellis Tree, please form chairs for our guests." Three branches pull themselves out of the trellis tree and weave themselves into chairs. Nana, Sam, and Maddie sit down as Sparks lies down at their feet.

In unison, Whitestar and Bluebell say, "We are Songmaster Souls. Our mission is to sing the New Earth into reality. On your present earth you would call us fairies."

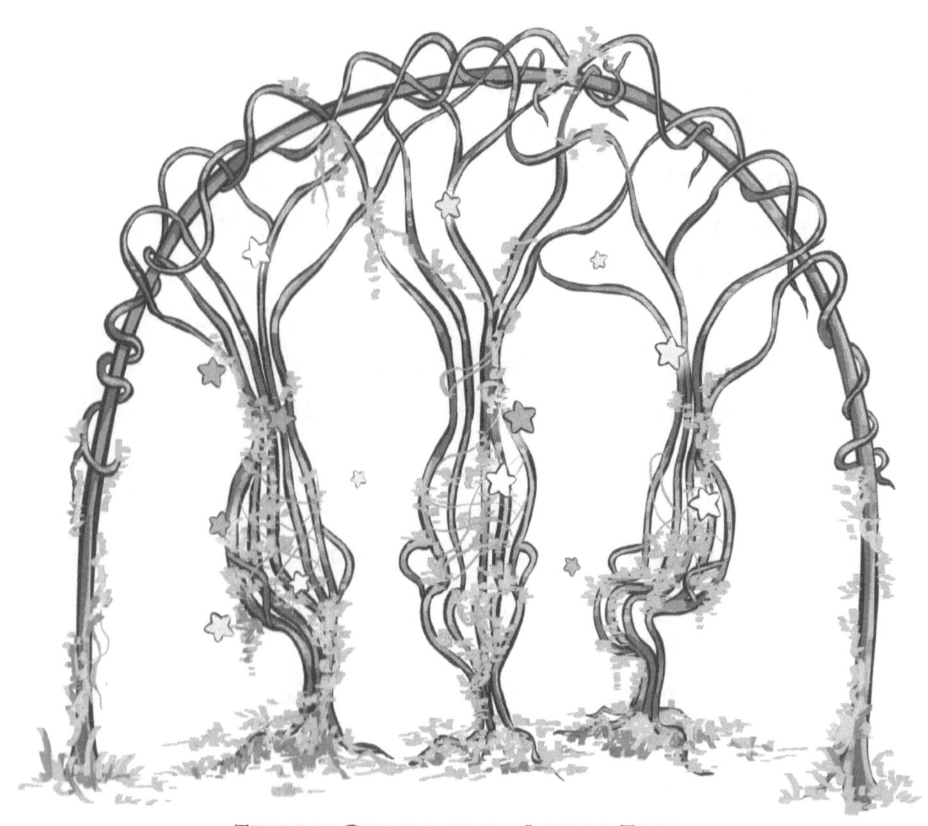

TRELLIS CHAIRS FROM LIVING TREE

"You are real! You are real! I knew you when I was little," exclaims Maddie. "Mom and Dad said you weren't real, and I needed to grow up."

"Yes, we can only be seen through the eyes of innocence," continues Whitestar. "In your world, as it is now, innocence is often destroyed by well-meaning but deeply wounded adults, who only know what their thoughts allow. We can only be perceived by the awe and wonder of a loving heart."

Bluebell adds, "Our songs support the amazing work going on underground, also facilitated by amazing leaders like Professor Schroom. Let me introduce you."

Suddenly, a three-foot-tall mushroom man appears before them, popping up from the ground of the riverbank. He bows as much as his bulbous body allows. Sparks jumps up too. "At your service, apprentices and canine friend. Let me tell you about the soil, my specialty! Diversity and reciprocity are the two keys to healthy soil!" booms Professor Schroom in a voice much louder than any of the new apprentices expected from his small body. Sparks watches the mushroom with a focused stare, his mouth closed and ears pricked forward, "The current practice of planting only one crop over and over on the same land is destroying the health of our soil. The nutrients in the soil

PROFESSOR SCHROOM

are depleted, and the soil structure and quality are weakened!" He takes a deep breath and is roaring now, "Destructive pests increase, and the pesticides used to kill these pests are poisonous. The health of all who rely on food grown from this dead soil are at risk, animals and humans alike. It's a royal mess! It must STOP!"

His booming voice fills the air. Sparks barks as if in agreement. "Professor Schroom is nothing if not passionate," whispers Nana, smiling.

"Creator has given us a perfect system of cooperation; everything works in reciprocity!" Professor Schroom says, in a voice so loving and respectful Sam wonders if he is going to burst into tears. "Let me show you."

With their inner eyes, Nana, Sam, and Maddie see a root. Around the root is a very thin halo. The halo covers every single hair on the root. "Every plant leaf is like a solar panel, capturing light and using it to turn carbon dioxide and water into oxygen and sugar, what you call photosynthesis," Professor Schroom croons adoringly. "Do you know what photosynthesis means?"

"Is that when you photoshop a fake photograph of yourself standing on the moon?" Maddie teases.

"No, photo means light; synthesis means to create a new thing out of several old things," Professor Schroom explains, ignoring her joke.

"These simple sugars form the building blocks of plants, but they are not enough. Plants also need nutrients like nitrogen and phosphorous from the soil, but they need help accessing them. Help comes from their beautiful friendship with bacteria, and fungi like me," Professor Schroom says affectionately.

"The plant releases sugars called exudates, secretions or oozy flows, in other words, through its roots. Bacterial colonies feed on the sugars, and the bacterial waste produces nutrients that the plant needs," he continues lovingly. "Isn't it beautiful how they all work together! Underground fungal networks called mycelium . . ." Professor Schroom pauses, "I see a questioning expression on your face, Maddie."

"Yes, Professor, what is mycelium?[22] I've never heard this word before. It sounds like where I would find the lightbulb in my room—on my celium."

Everyone laughs, except the Professor. Then he continues, "Ah yes, mycelium, my home body. We fungi live in a mass of fine-branching root-like tubes of white filaments. Our home bodies cover a huge area enjoying a vast range of nutrients and connecting multiple plants. We fungi symbiotically trade nutrients for the exudates as well."

Maddie adds, "What's 'symbiotically' mean? It sounds like the earache a cymbal player in the marching band might develop!"

"Oh no, my dear child—I understand why you—a very musical child I'm sure—might think so but such is not the case. Symbiosis means 'a mutually beneficial relationship between different organisms.'[23]

"The halo you see is the *rhizosphere*. This is where these reciprocal relationships happen and form the soil food web. THIS IS THE GRANDEST PARTNERSHIP IN LIFE ON EARTH!" Professor Schroom roars as his booming voice fills the air for miles around." Sparks runs around them all, his tail wagging joyously.[24]

"That's quite a voice for a mushroom," giggles Maddie quietly, "He roars like a rhino living in a rhinosphere."

"That's the rhizosphere; it's the halo-like area around the root where many bacteria and microorganisms feed on the sugars and proteins released by the root. It must be intact and healthy for life above ground to flourish. Mother Earth's systems are based on reciprocity, and farming practices must remember this for the earth to return to balance. WE MUST FARM LIKE NATURE DOES!" Professor Schroom exclaims as his bulbous body jumps up and down. When he finally slows down he says, "This lecture always wears me out. I must go now and hook up with my mycelium and recharge," and suddenly disappears.

"Professor Schroom is quite a character, isn't he?" observes Sam grinning from ear to ear as everyone chuckles. "Seems like a fun guy," laughs Nana.

"This is why we use a no-till method for our community gardens," Nana adds. "What happens in the soil is crucial to the nutrients in the food supply. The health of the food supply affects all of us who eat. Every living being on earth is connected both in the microcosm and macrocosm. When the soil is depleted, we are all depleted. Much of the soil on earth, as it is now, is depleted as well. We are a world out of balance. You could say we eat the soil for better or worse. Good soil, good food, I always say."

"Nana's community garden is a model for the New Earth," adds SilverLight, "and she is not alone. Galactic Guardians are creating such models all over the world. All life on earth is connected, and we must make decisions and act with this understanding to bring the earth back into balance."

All is quiet except for the sound of the bells, as Sam, Maddie, and Nana sit on living chairs amidst scents of joy, contemplating the oneness of life on earth and all its implications. Sparks rests at their feet, his tail wagging happily.

"I feel so good here," sighs Maddie. "I don't feel this way in school or certainly not at home." Nana reaches for Maddie's hand, holds it, and lovingly says, "I know your family is struggling now, Maddie."

"Your school's focus is on training the average mind," continues SilverLight. "The run-of-the-mill mind is an important tool for humans on earth, and it needs to be educated. However, love is seldom found in the average mind. That mind evaluates, judges, and separates into categories, very important skills for running a business or sending a rocket into space. However, the mind of the Mirror Dragon is a higher mind, one that is on fire with the breath of life—of imagination and the power to dream of a better future, the new world, in fact. It sees and understands the logic of unconditional love, unconditional acceptance, and inclusion and surrenders to it in joy. This higher mind, like the scales on my tail, becomes a mirror for love for all that is. The higher mind can reflect on every aspect of the multiverse at once, if it wishes but ultimately turns to the oneness of love for the true and correct answer—which is why those who know us call us Oneness dragons. Humans are destined to enter the oneness, too, but have a long way to go."

"What can we do?" asks Sam.

"Galactic Guardians have come to earth with gifts to give during this time of great change. What are your gifts? Look within and observe yourself in the world. What interests and skills do you have? If your heart is pure and you truly want to help bring the world back into balance, your steps will be guided," SilverLight says, "even if you can't always explain how you know what you know when you know it."

They are quiet for a while, then they each say, "Yes, I want to help."

"Thank you for your service," SilverLight, Bluebell, and WhiteStar say in unison.

A warm cozy mist envelopes them, and when it dissipates, Maddie, Sam, Nana, Sparks, and SilverLight are back at the Mother Tree in the forest.

"I'll take you both home now. Come over tomorrow for lunch, and we'll brainstorm our gifts. Give it some thought to-night," Nana says as they walk to her car.

"I can't tomorrow," Maddie responds. "Mother reminded me we need to clean the house tomorrow."

Although Sam can hardly wait to find out more about his possible future, he realizes that he has a soccer game the next day. "I have a soccer game tomorrow, and Mom asked me to help with cleaning and organizing Uplift the day after."

"Okay," Nana says, "Ask about two days after tomorrow and let me know."

Sam and Maddie nod their heads in agreement.

Dreamtime with Trees

Maddie falls into bed with her heart and mind full of all that has occurred. She's exhausted but has trouble falling asleep until Sparks nestles against her shoulder. When she finally does, SilverLight is waiting. "Your presence is requested. Bring your hollow gull bone." Maddie puts the bone in her pocket, jumps on SilverLight's back, and they take flight. Maddie senses moving through a tunnel and then, with a bright flash, entering another realm. "We have moved through a portal," SilverLight explains.

They land in front of a grove of giant trees and are greeted by two Tree People, the Ents. "Welcome!" they boom in their deep baritone voices. "Follow us!"

ENT

As Maddie crosses the entryway into the Sacred Grove, the light changes to filtered greens of every imaginable shade.

"Welcome to the Cathedral of the Ancient Ents," her guides croon.

She finds herself in an enormous hall enclosed by living trees. The trees come from every species and are woven together in intricate patterns and shapes forming both walls and ceiling. As she moves forward into the cavernous cathedral, her feet sink into soft leaves and mosses, and she finds herself dressed in a gown of leaves. She notices a hot spring winding along the edges of the cathedral-like space. The damp woodsy scents of moss, fallen leaves and pine needles send ripples of relaxation throughout her body!

She finally reaches the end of a long hall where two gigantic Ents are waiting. Her modestly-sized Ent guides announce, "Maddie, we present you to the Ancient Ents of the Cathedral." Maddie has to bend her head back as far as she can and look up to see their faces.

"Greetings, Little One. We name you The Listener, and we have a gift for you," they say, as a star is placed on top of Maddie's head.

When the star is placed on her head, all the trees in the cathedral light up. She sees streams of sparkling green light moving up from the tree's roots, lighting up the trunk and soaring into the cosmos. She also sees streams of crystalline light flowing down from the cosmos, into the leaves, down the trunk, and into the roots and soil.

"Trees are Mother Earth's wood-wide-web. The Standing Ones chat with terrestrial beings of the forest but also text with the Galactic Families of Light, our celestial relatives as well. We all come from the stars, as you now know." Maddie nods in agreement. "Trees send out both updates about the state of the earth and receive instant messages from those supporting us from above. Human's wanton destruction of both the forests and the soil has disrupted this process. However, there is hope. When two-legged Listeners are at one with the Standing Ones, the connections between above and below are amplified and strengthened once again. 'As Above So Below' is our motto."

Maddie bows, "Thank you, Ancient Ones. What else do I need to know about the mission of a Listener?"

"The mission is to open yourself to nature's ancient knowledge, Maddie the Listener, and share it with other humans. As you know, all of nature is sentient, capable of listening, each being according to its original blueprint. Many people, including your family, are not ready to hear from us though, and trying to share this knowledge with them may bring you distress. We will help you discern who is ready. Do you accept this mission?"

"Yes," Maddie answers.

"Thank you for your service, youngling. Now take a soaking in the hot springs, and you will wake up refreshed." Maddie is led to the hot springs and luxuriates in the warm, woodsy water until she awakens from her dream.

MADDIE THE LISTENER

Maddie wakes up to Sparks licking her right ear, then her left. "Good morning, Sparks! You've never licked my ears before. What's up?"

Sparks stares into her eyes and she hears, "I'm licking your ears because you have been newly born as Maddie the Listener."

"Ah, you know about my dream!" she exclaims as Sparks licks her ears again. She gives Sparks a good long belly rub and then gets dressed and goes into the kitchen.

The mood around Maddie's house this morning is calmer than usual. She makes cinnamon French toast for breakfast. Her dad grabs his with his thermos and leaves for work. "This is delicious, Maddie!" her mother comments as syrup drips down her face. "Yum, is there more?"

Maddie makes a second batch.

After breakfast, she dances through her housework and her mother notices. "You're doing a good job, Maddie, and you seem so happy."

"Mom, being with Nana and Sam makes me happy. If I work hard today, may I go to Nana's the day after tomorrow?"

"Yes, dear, I'm glad you're finding some friends here. I know moving's been pretty hard for you," and she gives Maddie a hug,

When Maddie is finished for the day, she puts the hollow gull bone in her jean's pocket, and she and Sparks go into the greenbelt behind her house. "Let's find the Douglas fir that Maple chose for me."

As Maddie enters the greenbelt, she is first aware of a feeling of sadness. A chipmunk scurries under her feet and she hears, "So many trees lost," and she is reminded that a forest was clear-cut to make room for her housing development. "I'm so sorry, Chipmunk," Maddie cries as the grief overtakes her. She sits down on the ground and prays. "Dear Forest and all who call this home, I am so sorry. I apologize for the humans who don't understand what they have destroyed, who don't understand they are destroying themselves too. I'm so sorry," and with tears streaming down her cheeks, she feels the need to make an offering, to give something back. She spontaneously takes her handmade beaded bracelet off her wrist and thinks of her grandmother. Her grandmother taught her how to string beads and make her first bracelet when she was seven, just before her grandmother died. Maddie has added beads to this bracelet as she has grown ever since. "My mother's mother and I give you this offering, made from our love."

A hummingbird flies right up to her face and the words enter her mind, "Thank you for your offering. The Indigenous People of this land always gave back. You must be a Galactic Guardian, one who understands the earth is sacred." She and Sparks follow the hummingbird through thickets of silal bushes to the foot of a giant Douglas fir surrounded by younger trees.

"Welcome. You can call me Dortha. Sit with me and feel Mother Earth's love for you," Maddie hears as she scans Dortha's broad trunk from roots to crown. She sits down with her back to Dortha, and Sparks crawls into her lap. She begins to weep. As she cries, she feels a liquid softness move from the ground up, and she quiets. "I love how alive I feel, Dortha, with all of this listening, but it's overwhelming."

"Look at the good you are already doing, Maddie. Your mother is warm and loving with you today. Your joy brings her out of her depression, at least for today. When you feel alive Maddie, you lighten the feelings of those around you. Love and joy are contagious! Chipmunk, Hummingbird, and I are also lightened when you listen to us. We feel more alive too!"

"I'm surprised to see such a big tree in our greenbelt."

"One of the developer's daughters is a Listener and knows how important Mother Trees are. She showed her dad Dr. Suzanne Simard's research on Mother Trees. He doesn't care about us, but he adores his daughter and was impressed with her knowledge, so I was spared. I can continue to nourish the younger trees and the surrounding ecosystem, although it is only a fraction of what it was and we are isolated, cut off by all the roads and homes. Much diversity was lost, and we are grieving. But we continue to fulfill our natures as best we can during these hurting times. Listeners like you help reconnect us, and we want to share our knowledge with you."

"I feel wonderfully alive, but how do I know this isn't my imagination?" Maddie wonders as she leans back into the tree's trunk.

"The proof is in how you feel, Maddie, and how others feel around you," Dortha answers telepathically.

"At least I know one of my gifts now and can tell Nana and Sam when we talk again," Maddie ponders. Now more deeply relaxed, she rests until it begins to get dark. Maddie and Sparks say goodbye to Dortha and walk home.

As Maddie and Sparks are walking from the forest patch, they pass the school's secondary soccer field and run into Sam in his soccer uniform. His eyes are red and puffy, his face crimson, and his shoulders slumped.

"Hi Sam, is everything all right?"

"Hi Maddie. No, it's not! I tripped on the ball during the final minutes of the game—stepped right on it, and I went flying! What's worse is the ball went spinning right into the path of the other team's best player! He turned it around and scored the winning goal!"

"Oh, that must have been humiliating for you!"

"Oh yes, indeed! I feel terrible. Now my dreams of being captain are trashed for good!"

"Not necessarily, Sam. Come on. Everyone knows you are the best player on the team. It could happen to anyone."

"You think?"

"Yeah. You know the Mother Tree and friends just recognized me as a good listener. I need some practice. Do you want to help me listen? I might make mistakes."

"Okay, I guess."

"I will hold space for you," they both hear SilverLight say as she surrounds them with her healing silver mist.

Sam and Maddie walk together to a large rock at the edge of the field and sit down. Maddie says, "So tell me what happened. I'm listening!"

"Well, it was a tie game and coming up on 85 minutes. You know a game is 90 minutes long, right? Anyway, the other team was charging downfield towards the goalposts to tee up and score what would have been the winning point. I got a foot on it, but I was too clumsy and off balance, and the ball started rolling towards the sideline. I thought, 'If it goes out of play it will be their ball, because of my mistake, and that will give them a winning advantage.' I got scared and ran as fast as I could towards the sideline to get in front of the ball and give it a big heel kick. But I tensed up and stepped right on top of the ball instead. I did keep it in play, but I went flying out of bounds instead. The ball spun to the side and landed right in front of Nasty Ned Northcutt, the other team's best player. He dribbled towards the goalposts and swerve-kicked it into the net for the winning point. Our goalie fell on it but was helpless to stop it. That was it!"

"You mean you tried a heel kick save? Doesn't this require a great deal of practice and skill? And you actually kept the ball in play? I'm impressed!"

Sam answers, sadly, "I watched the videos on how to do it and practiced it at home. I want to be the best. I want to be captain."

"Sam, it takes more than watching videos to master soccer. Just like life, you learn from experience and, of course, lots of practice!"

"But I do practice . . ."

Maddie says, "I hear you. I hear your pain and your heartbreak. But I imagine that big game experience is a lot different than backyard experience. Do you agree?"

"Yes, of course."

"And how many heel kicks have you made this season in real games so far?"

"None, yet, at least no good ones."

"So that's great. You got your feet wet. You tasted the big time. You get an A for effort. What did you learn from this experience?"

"I misjudged the speed of the ball and didn't extend my leg far enough. I won't do that again!"

"Okay, what else?"

"I let myself get nervous. It was a big game, a big moment. How do you practice not being nervous in a big game?"

"Why not ask SilverLight about this. She's right here. Let's close our eyes and call upon her." They both close their eyes and SilverLight appears almost immediately in their mind's eye.

"Greetings, sports fans. How can I help?" asks SilverLight.

Maddie says, "Sam here needs help staying calm in the middle of a big game. What would you recommend?"

"This nervousness can happen when you think too much like a human, all this worrying about what other people think, and what's going to happen in the future. Your mind is all over the place. No focus! You need to think like a dragon. Sam, I'm going to allow you to mind-meld with me for just a moment. Is this all right?"

"You bet."

"Okay, here we go. Slowly pull in the reins on your brain. Make the map smaller. Forget everything you hear on the news, things other students say in the hallways, or worries about grades. Forget the videos. Forget about clock time. Narrow the focus. Just be! Can you feel my dragon brain merging with yours? We are centered on the Now. No fear. No fear of failure or judgment. We are starting over from scratch. Can you find a part of yourself that is not a projected desire or fear but is the being that has those desires?"

"Yes!"

"Does this being want to express itself?"

"Yes."

"What does it want to express?"

"Greatness."

"Exactly. Isn't this part of you already great?"

"Yes, actually, it is. My true self, my spirit, my soul, or whatever, higher self, is great and has always been great, and will always be great. I just want to express this in my life!"

"What's stopping you?"

"I don't have the skills. I need to learn the skills and then put them into action. Not only in soccer but in everything I do."

"Visualize the ball rolling out of bounds."

"Okay. It's rolling."

"Now slow it down.

"It's slowing."

"Now leap ahead of it in slow motion, land on one foot, and then clearly visualize yourself giving the ball a good heel kick to keep it in bounds. Not to please your teammates or coach Hadley or the fans. Just as a way to express your greatness."

"Okay, here goes! I'm leaping, in slow motion. I land. I kick. BOOM! I give it a masterful heel kick. It is a thing of beauty! Everyone cheers."

"Don't worry about the cheering, Sam. Remember, you are finding yourself as a dragon, not trying to please others. You are expressing yourself as a soccer artist. It's not about winning. You are showing your dragon fire."

SilverLight turns her head to the right, and in illustration of her point, she belches a huge stream of smoke and fire across her right shoulder, above the field of weeds and reeds. Some of the reeds seem to wilt with the heat of her breath.

"You start getting hooked on the cheering part and your head will get too big and I'll have to disconnect from you. That's not what greatness is about. It's about learning the skills so that you can express through your body, your physical life, whatever is in your heart. Then you can achieve your dreams. Now let's go over this heel kick again. Visualize this move a second time and a third time. I'm here with you. You can tap into my power as a Master Dragon if it helps you. Maddie is here as a witness as well."

Sam goes through the same heel kick visualization two more times in slow motion. "Okay, I have it now. But how do I keep from getting nervous in a game?"

"Stop thinking so much. Stay in the moment. That's where your dragon power is."

Maddie says, "This concludes our visualization exercise. I hope you found it useful. You can open your eyes now." They both do so. Their shared visions of SilverLight disappear.

Maddie says, "Wait a minute, Sam. See that long track of blackened weeds and reeds, over there to our left? Was that there when we arrived?"

Sam answers, "My eyes were filled with tears at that moment. I mighta missed it! But, no, I don't remember it being there before."

Maddie places the side of her hand in front of her mouth and ducks her head, her habitual "don't kill me" gesture, and says, "Oooops!"

"How do you feel now, Sam?" Maddie asks.

"Much better," Sam replies, and he feels much closer to both Maddie and SilverLight as they get up to leave. "Thank you!"

SAM THE LEADER

"Time to wake up," Sarah yells from the kitchen.

"Okay, Mom!" Sam answers as he stretches and slowly gets out of bed. He's a little sore after yesterday's soccer game. He smells cinnamon as he walks into the kitchen.

"Do you want oatmeal or eggs with your cinnamon toast?" Sarah asks.

"Oatmeal, please!" As Sarah sets the bowl down, Sam asks, "What's needed at Uplift today, Mom?"

"Are you okay, Sam? You sound weary," Sarah asks.

"Had a rough game yesterday. I'll get over it."

"It's a perfect day for you to volunteer, Sam. The high school students with special needs transitioning into the workplace are coming today."

"You finally got permission?" Sam mumbles with a mouthful of cereal.

"Yes, it took months, and your father's anger at the injustice of it all helped light a fire under their feet. I still don't understand the school's objections to the students visiting and working with us. These young people have a variety of mobility and cognitive issues and need accommodations but make wonderful employees, if trained. Your father just wouldn't take no for an answer. When he started quoting the Individuals with Disabilities Education Act, he just wore them down, I think!" she giggles. "The students are visiting possible job sites. I'd love to have several of them choose to work with us. They are reliable workers. We just have to structure the tasks at their comfort level. Today we will show them how to sort clothes donations."

After breakfast, Sarah and Sam drive to Uplift. There are colorful flags and kites blowing in the wind at the entrance. "So joyful and inviting," Sam thinks. They park by the drive-up drop-off station by the garage door. There is a buzzer at car window level, and when pressed, a worker comes out to accept the donations and write a receipt. Every aspect is designed with convenience in mind.

When they walk into the garage, they see large vats and shelving for grouped items such as clothing, housewares, toys, tools, etc. As they enter the main store, Sam sees volunteers working at the repair and reuse station in the back of the store, fondly called "The Dare to Repair Café" or sometimes the "The Fix-It Farm." Volunteers with the needed skills come three times a week to repair customers' appliances, tools, and technology. "Our little way of curbing waste and saving our customers' money," Sarah always says.

They hear voices at the entrance and see ten students and three school staff entering and with them are Maddie, Sparks, and others from her therapy dog class with their dogs. Sam and Maddie wave at each other across the room. Sarah notices three students are in wheelchairs. "I'll get a table at the level of the wheelchairs," she says as she walks off. She comes back rolling a long table and sets it up by a vat brimming with donated clothes. As the students make their way to the worktable, the therapy dogs move from student to student, offering cuddles and kisses.

Everyone is working well until loud, angry voices erupt. The staff starts to approach the arguing students, but Sam arrives first. "Let's see how Sam handles this," Sarah says, motioning the staff back. Sam places his hands gently on the angry students' shoulders and talks to them quietly for a few minutes, then everyone happily goes back to work.

"He's quite a leader, isn't he," comments a school staff member standing off to the side with Sarah.

"Yes, he's always been so; not much shakes him. A soccer friend challenged him a few days ago in a menacing way. The friend taunted, 'I have lots of friends besides you!' Sam simply said, 'Wonderful! It's great to have lots of friends.' The menacing tone didn't even register. Last year he received an award in karate. An older child came up and taunted him, 'My award is higher than yours!' Sam didn't even notice. He just celebrated with the other students who had received awards. He keeps a positive attitude that focuses on the good, and it brightens our home. We are so blessed."

It's almost lunchtime when a huge explosion rocks the building. The dogs begin to bark. Everything sways as items fall off shelves and break. Everyone in the building is in shock, and some of the students start to cry. Staff at the entrance go outside and see a building two doors down engulfed in flames. "Fire!" they yell, pointing to the left.

Sam looks up and sees a framed picture of a barn owl, just like Owl from the forest. He hears Owl say, "Remember your promise, Sam. You were made for this." Then he sees the faint outline of SilverLight filling the building with a cooling mist. Sam feels himself grow bigger and stronger inside and announces in a commanding voice, "Follow me!" All the regular volunteers are familiar with the emergency evacuation route.

Sam leads the school staff, students, and therapy teams out a side door further away from the fire, and they walk several blocks away where their school bus is waiting. Maddie gives Sam a hug and whispers, "Good job," before she and Sparks enter the bus with the students. Meanwhile, Sarah makes sure everyone is out of Uplift and gives the firemen her contact information and keys to the building. "I'll take my son home, then come back to lock up when you give the go-ahead."

"I'm proud of you, Sam. You are a true leader, the kind of leader people want to follow," Sarah says as they get into the car.

"Thanks, Mom," Sam says as he thinks, "I will tell Nana and Maddie that leadership is one of my gifts. If I'm going to be a soccer team captain, I need to practice thinking like one and accept leadership as one of my gifts."

Although the incident is not a forest fire, due to the relatively dry conditions, everyone is on high alert, ready to perform emergency duties as planned. The fire does not reach Uplift, although many items are broken and some with smoke damage must be discarded. Everyone is just grateful no one was hurt.

Nana hears about the fire and is at Sam's house when Sarah and Sam arrive. Maddie and Sparks arrive a few minutes later. "I just needed to be with you after all of this," Maddie explains. "Me too" says Nana. They all sit down together. Nana is in a wistful mood and begins to weave tales about the wisdom of nature.

"You know leaders will emerge from this fire; they always do. It brings out the courage in people. They are like salamanders, those amphibious creatures that, in the old days, were associated with fire. Salamanders would hide in rotten logs for days, and as soon as someone would throw the log onto a roaring fire, salamanders would come crawling out looking for a safer place to live. So, they imagined salamanders were created out of fire, at least in the old stories. Salamanders are not really reptiles; they are born with gills, not lungs, and are born in water. Reptiles lay eggs on land and are born with lungs."

Maddie perks up, eyes shining like a puppy. "Dragons create eggs, but they don't lay them! SilverLight told us she and her partner create them together out of love and intention. They are energetic beings who take on whatever shape is needed. They take on the reptile shape for humans."

Nana continues, "Did you know that millions of years ago in what is now Australia, in the Mesozoic era, (meso means middle, zoic pertains to animals and other creatures) there was a flying reptile, a dinosaur we call a Pterosaur? Today we still have the Chinese Water Dragon, which lays eggs, but looks more like an iguana. Some salamanders look like dragons, but as amphibians, they are less closely related."

Sam asks, "What about whales? Are they related to dinosaurs?"

Nana smiles, "Probably. But their land-striding ancestors appeared about 50 million years ago, long after dinosaurs disappeared, and yes, they might have been related."

"Cool! Who were these walking whales?"

"There are many kinds of whales, and they developed out of several different land mammals. The Pakicetus lived in what is now Pakistan and India. It lived near the water and loved to eat fish. There was some sort of climate disaster even back then, and so it eventually moved to the underwater world and became some type of whale."

"Wow. Were there others?"

"Yes. Some evolved from the Artiodactyl at about the same time. Millions of years later, the Dorudon, the size of a goat, developed a feeding filter in its mouth like most whales have today. There may have been other whale ancestors on land. Did you know whales still breathe oxygen like you do? They just hold their breath a very long time."

"Are dragons related to whales?" Maddie asks.

"Not really. Dragons, if they existed on earth, must have been like reptiles, whereas all whales are mammals. They are on different branches of the tree of biological life. But some people say that both whales and dragons are highly evolved souls, very ancient and very wise—and very, very large. In the old mythological tales, they both can be very helpful, or very destructive. Now it's getting late; time for all us ancient creatures to go to bed."

"Nana, you know EVERYTHING!" Maddie giggles.

"I've read a few books," Nana says as she stands up to leave. "Maddie, can I give you and Sparks a ride home?"

SEA DREAMS

That night, all three dream of the sea.

Maddie dreams she is riding a whale whose sonar sings,

"Come to the sea to deeply see.
Come to the sea to feel more free."

Sam dreams he shape-shifts into a dolphin and is swimming with his pod as their sonar sings,

"Unity Community, Unity Community,
Joyfully join us in Unity Community."

Nana dreams she has prepared a huge picnic. She's prepared food for herself and the children but is also feeding the many whales and dolphins who are surrounding her raft for their protection.

WHAT IS YOUR GIFT?

The next morning Sarah and Sam pick up Maddie and Sparks and drive to Nana's. "Have fun," Sarah says as they get out of the car. "We will!" they say in unison.

When they step inside Nana's, they smell cookies baking. "I'm in the kitchen," she yells. Sam and Maddie look at each other, laugh and say, "Of course!"

As they enter the kitchen, Nana sets a plate of warm cookies on the table and gives Sparks a dog biscuit. "Milk, water, or lemonade?" As she hears their preferences and fills their mugs, she continues, "I dreamt of you two last night," and she shares her raft picnic dream.

"I dreamt of the sea too," Maddie and Sam echo. They recount their dreams, then sit silently for several minutes, struck by the synchronicity.

Nana is the first to speak, "I've been thinking about my gifts, have you?" Maddie and Sam nod yes, and Sam says, "You go first, Nana."

"I am an educator and community organizer. Our model community garden teaches regenerative agriculture, and my role as community organizer grows naturally from the many groups that meet here. I feel Creator moves through me when I do this work."

"What's, er, 'regenerative' mean?" Maddie wonders aloud.

"Look at the word within the word. To regenerate means to generate or produce anew. Regenerative agriculture brings fertility back to damaged land. Here is our community brochure, Maddie," Nana replies as she hands it to Maddie.

Maddie opens the brochure and reads aloud, "Regenerative agricultural systems cooperate with nature. They draw down carbon, conserve water, replenish waterways, grow healthier food, reduce the use of harmful chemicals, employ people within the community, and ensure long-term vitality of the land."[25]

"Seems to me we've taken cooperating with nature to a whole new level," Maddie begins, then shares her dream adventure with the Ents.

"You are a Listener, Maddie, and your bond with trees and animals is amazing. Your friend Maple would be proud," Nana says warmly as a tear falls down Maddie's face.

"How about you, Sam?" Maddie asks, and Sam tells them about how his experience at Uplift helped confirm for him his abilities as Leader. "I want to be captain of my soccer team someday, but real leadership builds from within."

"Well, we have an Educator/Organizer, a Listener, and a Leader. Now what?" wonders Sam as the light in the room begins to shimmer and SilverLight appears. Sam, Maddie, and Nana gasp as SilverLight's reflective scales encompass Nana's entire home.

Sam gulps, "How big are you?"

"As big as I choose to be in any given moment," SilverLight roars, "limited only by my own thoughts and feelings." Sam, Maddie, and Nana stand amazed, while Sparks runs in circles, wagging his tail joyously.

"Well, now that I have your attention," laughs SilverLight, "If you're up for an adventure, I'd like to take you back into the Realm of Possibilities. First, I'll fly you to our hatchery; you can meet my eggs, and I'll show you around our outpost. The Realm of Possibilities holds all the blueprints needed for a more peaceful earth, and they are just waiting to be accessed. I'll show you one of the blueprints for a human community living in harmony with nature. Agreed?"

They all answer with a resounding "Yes!" as the Song of Innocence sailboat comes into view.

"Sing your songs and board," SilverLight croons as she sings love to her eggs.

As they sing their Songs of Innocence, the sailboat rises, and they are surrounded by a mist of luminous love. "I could stay here forever," murmurs Nana. After a while, they begin to descend, and when the mist dissolves, they find themselves in a humongous dragon's nest reaching as far as their eyes can see. Sparks stays very close to Maddie.

DRAGON OUTPOST

There are a multitude of celestial beings surrounding the enormous nest; they are so tall their heads merge with the sky. When Sam, Maddie, and Nana crook their necks back, they see waves of energy emanating from them. The waves are saturating the atmosphere with celestial chimes and feelings of love and joy. As the waves hit the eggs, the eggs hum, and a few eggs rock.

"We dragons are beings of pure-hearted love. The Celestial Beings are activating this blueprint within each egg. These galactic beings come from many different races and are here to support us. The eggs belong to my partner and me," Silver-Light says telepathically, as she gently touches each one with her snout. "The ones that are rocking will hatch soon. I always have part of my awareness here, so I can be totally present when they emerge."

Each egg is unique. There are blue, red, green, pearlescent, rainbow, and crystalline ones. As Nana gazes into SilverLight's tender, love-filled eyes, she is overcome with emotion. Maddie finds a tissue in her jacket pocket and quietly slips it to her. Nana wipes away a tear.

"Once the hatchlings can stand, they are taken to play school where they learn about their gifts and how to utilize them on earth. Let me show you. Best you climb on my back. It will take you forever to get there with your tiny legs," chuckles SilverLight.

After a short flight through the nest, SilverLight lands, and they climb down. They are standing in the midst of swirling dragonettes. Everyone is in motion. Some are taking off, others landing. Some are disappearing, others appearing. Some are breathing fire while others exhale a silver cooling mist.

"It feels so light and playful here," Maddie notices as she watches Sparks run among the dragonettes.

"Yes, Maddie, playfulness is the most powerful way to learn. You humans work too hard."

"True," agrees Nana. "Even our preschools are affected. They used to be 'come and play' schools. Now too many are just 'come sit and stay' schools, and kids are force-fed academics. We're twisting our children away from their true creative natures. It's devastating for them and our future."

"All the answers to your problems on earth are here, in the Realm of Possibilities," SilverLight resumes, "in the form of unhatched ideas. The blueprints for a joyful, health-filled life on earth exist, but you must have a little creativity to turn them into a reality. Only humans with pure intentions can access them. You must let go of your personal desires for power over others, wealth, and fame. For only those with a desire to improve the greater good for all will be allowed to enter." They all stand quietly while dragonettes of every possible color fly over their heads and under their legs, appearing and disappearing.

"They appear and disappear in a nanosecond!" Nana exclaims.

Sam, becoming swept up in the word game Maddie is playing says, "Nana-second, the time it takes my grandma to answer a question."

"Or a billionth of a second or a very short time," adds Nana playfully.

"Where is your partner, SilverLight, and what promise did you make to Creator?" Sam wonders.

"We dragons are Energy Masters, Sam. As you know, everything is energy. The heaviest objects in your world are just vibrating atoms with lots of space within them. It's your human sense organs that perceive certain vibrations as solid. Vibrating energy is our playground, and these young dragons are learning how to play.

"Our galactic dragon family is volunteering to support Mother Earth during Her birthing process. She is evolving and inviting all her relations to evolve with Her. Your beautiful earth was created out of love, but 'power-over' forces have derailed her path. We are part of a major course correction. My partner works on an interspecies galactic council overseeing this process. His role is to make sure our actions are in line with the universal laws Creator intended."

"How does he do this?" ponders Nana.

"By surrendering his personal hopes and dreams, wishes and desires, and emptying himself of all but the purest intention to serve Creator and the greatest good for all. We all strive for this, of course, but if he loses focus and forgets these intentions, we all feel it, and things start to go wrong. This is the other side of leadership."

Sam says, "This is what my coach says about being a team captain. He says this person needs to understand the needs and concerns of the whole team and place them ahead of personal goals. He says the captain needs to be a steady and calming influence and set a positive example for the players. This means positive, constructive communication at all times with teammates and coaches. He says the team captain should be lifting teammates up, not putting them down.[26]

"He said, 'This team has a chance for the junior varsity playoffs, and we could really use a team captain, but are any of you really capable of filling those big 'ol shoes?' Coach Hadley's a tough old bird and a former team captain, and I suddenly lost confidence in myself and let the challenge go unanswered."

SilverLight says, "You have some big games coming up, Sam. My soccer dragons and I will help you, not with winning, no, but with expanding your field of awareness so as to help you become a better player and leader. A good captain is able to think several plays ahead, and also several yards to each side, to know not only where the ball *is* at every moment, but where it *could be*. This means knowing where fellow players are, too, so he or she can pass to them, and also knowing where the best players on the other team are standing in case they can be sidestepped. All good leaders develop similar broad fields of awareness. Next game—I'll show you a few moves of my own. No one can head a ball into the net like a dragon."

All motion stops. A deep quiet settles over the playground as SilverLight's words infuse the air. Then she continues, "We dragons are each unique, just like you two-leggeds. We have individual gifts and missions as well. All of us can play in all the elements. We can all breathe fire to clear denser energies and lighten things up.

"However, we have our specialties, as well, according to our elemental categories. Fire dragons clear what is not aligned with the divine plan and lighten vibrational frequencies. Water dragons specialize in inspiring feelings of love and keeping our emotions light and joyful. They also hold space for possibilities to manifest. Air dragons focus on keeping thoughts clear and keeping the vibration of life pure. Earth dragons guard the physically manifested realms. Related to them are the Healer dragons who help keep the natural world in balance. They breathe a cool, soothing mist, and their claws activate energy meridians. I'm a Master Dragon. I have integrated all the elemental specialties and help them work together. To do this, I have to be in good health, physically, emotionally, mentally, and spiritually, which means I have to take good care of myself and keep my mirrors bright and shiny.

"I'm also a scout for our human ground crew. More two-leggeds who are pure of heart and listen within are needed.

Creator gave you the capacity to be in kinship *with* and stewards *of* the plants and animals of this beautiful earth. It's time to step into who you were created to be." Once again, they are quieted, as they let SilverLight's words sink in. "Now, the young dragons and I have created a little presentation for you. Watch and enjoy!"

"Dragons protect!" SilverLight calls out reminding Sam of a beloved Karate instructor he once trained with. First, the young dragons open their wings wide and spread them around themselves. Then they form a wider and wider circle until they are one body, encompassing each other and the visitors within their wingspan.

"Dragons rejoice!" The dragonettes dissolve into dancing multi-colored points of light. They swirl and twirl, appear and disappear at a faster and faster pace until their light-filled joy explodes up into the stars. "Look at Sparks!" Maddie exclaims. "She's running in the pattern of an infinity symbol!" Sam, Maddie, and Nana are filled with awe and wonderment as the presentations are completed.

ARRIVING AT THE ECOVILLAGE

"Best we move on," SilverLight advises after the presentations are completed. "You humans need to get your feet back on the ground to stay balanced. However, I do want to show you one of our ecovillage blueprints before we return. Climb on my back."

The four climb on SilverLight's back, and she takes off. They fly low to the ground, rising now and then to avoid collisions with trees and an assortment of other beings. A settlement comes into view.

"I'll give you an aerial view first. What do you see?"

"I see a large circle of colorful houses," Maddie volunteers.

"There is a huge garden in the middle of the circle," Nana says admiringly.

"All the houses have solar panels on the roofs," Sam notices with interest.

"Look, each house has a garden plot too!" adds Nana excitedly.

"Yes, this beautiful settlement sits on reclaimed land. We will land now, and I will tell you about its history. I will land just outside the circle of homes. There's a clearing there large enough for me."

When SilverLight lands and the three slide off her back, someone is waiting for them.

"Professor Schroom!" all three exclaim at once.

"At your service, once again, apprentices, stewards of the new world, and canine friend," he says with a bow. "I am here to tell you the history of this soil! Follow me," and he shouts and leads them towards the settlement. "SilverLight, are you going to stay out here or shrink?"

"I'll stay out here for now. I want to tune into my eggs, but I'll stay in touch with your tour telepathically."

The three walk beside Professor Schroom, but a three-foot mushroom does not move quickly, and they are all just creeping along. "This will take forever," Maddie whispers to Sam.

"Friend Raven, I need a lift," shouts Professor Schroom, and a huge raven lands in front of the Professor. The Professor climbs on Raven's back and calls out, "Follow us!"

"Now we have to run to keep up!" pants Maddie.

Raven lands and lets the Professor off at the edge of the community garden. The Professor bows, "Thank you, my friend," and Raven bows three times in response.

Professor Schroom bends down and takes a handful of soil. "This beautiful soil was subjected to such great violence. You kids might not be able to see the scars, but I do! So sad! In order to grow a lot of one crop, it was tilled over and over again. Oh my, oh my, such a travesty. My dear rhizosphere and all the soil's structure were broken into little bits. The carbon dioxide the soil kept in store was released into the air. No soil structure, no water retention, dreadful erosion, and the fungi and bacteria were slaughtered, *slaughtered*, I tell you!" Tears began to stream out of Professor Schroom's pores. "And if this wasn't enough destruction, the land was sprayed with chemicals to kill the pests, but there are so many more beneficial insects massacred at the same time, and you eat those chemicals. They get in the water, and you drink them. So, so stupid! When will humans wake up! It's just too much! Excuse me for a moment; I must collect myself."

Maddie starts to offer the Professor a tissue but decides a mushroom might not have use for one.

"Okay, okay," the Professor says catching his breath. "Now for the good news—the healing process that eventually brought this soil back to life! Mother Earth is the ultimate healer, but we must honor the reciprocal relationships inherent in healthy soil. Never leave the soil uncovered. Plant cover crops high in the nutrients needed and rotate them each season. Prioritize native plants which draw beneficial insects and don't use chemical insecticides. Roll the cover crops over each season, but never till. It took seven years, but finally, all the biological players returned here to do their part. When the microbes once again created the glue that holds these soil particles together, and the rhizosphere and mycelium were back in business, there was a huge party down there! Soil resurrection! I AM PROFESSOR SCHROOM AND I APPROVE OF THIS SOIL!"

"And carbon sequestration can draw down greenhouse gases," adds Nana.

"What is sea-quest-ration?" asks Sam. "It sounds like when Odysseus went on a quest to the sea," teases Sam keeping the wordplay going.

"To sequester means to isolate or hide away," Nana explains.

"And why do green-painted houses need gasoline," asks Sam with a wry smile.

Nana answers in a nanosecond, "Gasses such as carbon dioxide and methane are increased by us humans burning too much gasoline, and that causes the so-called greenhouse effect!"

"What's the greenhouse effect?" Sam asks.

Nana says, "A glass greenhouse in your yard keeps the plants warm in winter—and very warm in summer. Our overuse of fossil fuels like gasoline cause our atmosphere to hold in all the warmth, and it heats up the plants—and the oceans— melting the ice caps at the north and south poles, which turn into water, thus causing sea levels to rise."

"Yes, the sun's energy stimulates the plant to absorb carbon dioxide through photosynthesis. The CO2 is moved through the cells and is stored in plant tissue, as well as soil organisms who feed on the exudates, secretions, or oozy flow in other words, from the roots. When the organisms die, the carbon is stored deep in the soil," explains the Professor.

A stillness fills the air for a few moments as the visitors digest this information. Then Professor Schroom continues, "I'm exhausted. I need to go hook up with my mycelium again, and recharge. Bye for now!"

"Thank you, Professor Schroom, for a most enlightening presentation," Nana says bowing to the mushroom. Maddie and Sam follow suit and before they are finished, Professor Schroom disappears in a flash, downwards, back into the soil.

TOURING THE ECOVILLAGE

Two young people, about Maddie and Sam's age, approach. "Welcome apprentices, those who love and protect the earth, we are your guides. Let us show you our ecovillage. Please come with us. As you can see," they continue, taking turns talking as they lead the visitors around the village, "homes are situated in a circle surrounding communal gardens. Every home has solar panels on its roof. The technology has progressed to the point that even cloudy days produce energy. All windows with access to the sun are also made of clear solar panels. These solar window panels are just being discovered in your time.[27] We only use bikes and small solar-powered vehicles like your golf carts when we don't want to walk within our community. We do have larger solar-powered vehicles and low-flying solar aircraft for trips away. They are housed in garages and hangars behind the homes, but we plan our trips carefully, so we don't overuse our fuel. Planning our trips more efficiently starts with planning our lives and communities more efficiently as well. We work with the earth, not against it.

"Between each home is a 9' x 12' garden plot. Each family is responsible for their plot. Trees were clear-cut here years ago, so we have planted new ones. We considered the garden's needs for sun in their placement. Some plots are full sun and others are partly shaded. Each spring, we meet and each family decides what it wants to grow. We do our best to have a variety because, during market days, we can trade what we grow for something we need.

"The communal garden in the middle of the circle of homes is cared for by all," the guides continue as they all enter a community building. "Here is the work board. Residents can choose to plant, harvest, water, collect seeds, turn over the compost pile, etc. For those who aren't able-bodied, there are tasks such as shelling peas and snapping the ends off the green beans. Everyone contributes. As soon as toddlers can walk, they are given small watering cans and other tasks in the garden. The more time we spend supporting the garden, the more produce we can pick. We also have an 'offer/ask' board. Each resident can both offer a skill they are willing to give and ask for help with a need they have.

"When we have a question or consider a change of some kind, we consult with All Our Relations who share this land with us, the trees, plants, and animals. We are in harmony with nature and can consult the elements as well."

"Where are your schools?" asks Nana.

"Mostly out in nature. Classes are held outdoors most of the year. It all comes down to planning ahead. We offer our children lots of experiences and encourage them to follow their joy. Their joy leads them to their gifts. See that banner over there?" They all look to a colored banner stretching across the eastern wall. It reads: *Be true to your inner nature. We are each a vital piece of the whole.*

"Do you have livestock?" Sam asks.

"We have a tractor that moves the chicken coop from place to place where a portable fence is set up for 3–4 days. The chickens provide needed fertilizer—as their poop is extremely high in nitrogen, and they eat termites, slugs, ticks, hookworms, and more. They provide eggs for breakfast as well! We also have a herd of goats that provide milk, clear brush, and offer us endless entertainment. Goats really know how to play! We seldom eat meat, but if someone needs it, we ask an animal to offer itself. A chicken or goat will come forward, and we honor it in every way possible during its sacrifice, preparation, and eating."

"Where are your dogs?" they all hear Sparks ask telepathically.

"Sparks! You can talk to us?" Nana and Sam ask in unison.

"Of course," Sparks says with a chuckle in his voice. "Here in the Realm of Possibilities I have lots to say! You humans need to slow down, and pay attention to the simple things in life. Quiet your minds, calm down, and cuddle more!" Everyone is silent for a few moments, absorbing Sparks' words.

"Families choose the kind of animal friends they want, and animals are a big part of our outdoor school. They have a lot to teach us!" continue the guides.

As the visitors are shown around, they are amazed at how joyful the residents are. When they comment on it, their guides recite in unison, "Thank you, Sun. Thank you, Rain. Healthy soil breeds a healthy, happy human. So love the land and it will love you back!" and they laugh. "This is our pledge of allegiance. The children recite it every school day, and we do too before every meeting."

"I'm tired," admits Nana. "This is a lot to take in."

"Let's feed you before you return," their guides offer. They call to a young boy, "Ask the community kitchen to bring us a picnic, please." The young boy runs off and soon returns with a basket full of hard-boiled eggs, goat cheese, and fruit. The young people and Sparks share food and conversation while Nana closes her eyes for a while.

RETURNING TO NANA'S

"Time to return," they hear SilverLight say telepathically. After many warm hugs and goodbyes, the trio returns to where SilverLight is waiting, and mount. "Thanks, SilverLight. This was mind-blowing, to say the least," Sam utters, "I'm beginning to get the whole picture!"

"Wholeness is what it's all about, my friend," the dragon says. "By now you are just beginning to understand. It's not this or that or the other thing that matters most. It's the wholeness that matters. That's what we all need to take good care of. Whenever a forest is lost, the earth loses a bit of wholeness. Whenever whales beach themselves and die, a part of the wholeness is lost."

Sam replies, "Whales seem to have a wholeness about them that humans don't, at least not anymore. They seem complete within themselves."

Maddie chimes in, "And there's only one letter difference!!"

"What?"

"You know! Whale! Change the 'a' to an 'o' and it spells whole!" Maddie explains, as if revealing some esoteric secret.

"Oh, I never thought of that," Sam responds. "In any case, shouldn't we be getting back home now?"

"Your wish is my command, apprentices, shapers of the New Earth, if the wish is for the benefit of all sentient beings!" the dragon replies as they take off. Soon they are back in Nana's home on earth and SilverLight announces excitedly, "I must go now, my eggs are hatching. They are calling to me!"

As SilverLight slowly disappears, the trio yells, "Congratulations," in unison.

"Whew!" Sam sighs. "What now?" They sit speechlessly for several minutes.

Maddie starts absentmindedly humming,

"Come to the sea to deeply see.
Come to the sea to feel more free."

Then Sam joins in,

"Unity Community, Unity Community
Joyfully join us in Unity Community."

"Ah yes, what now? I think last night's dreams about whales, dolphins, and the sea answer that question," answers Nana. "We need to visit the Cetacean Human Partnership Institute."

Maddie and Sam look puzzled. Maddie asks, "What planet is *that* on?"

Nana winks and says, "Would you believe Earth? Well, Washington State, actually. The CHP Institute is in the San Juan Islands in the Salish Sea. The researchers include renowned cetologists, as well as Native Americans whose cultures and traditions are deeply connected with our local dolphins and whales.

"I know one of the researchers there. When his gifted son was a teenager, he had a fear of standardized tests. I helped him get over this, and I am proud to say he just finished his Ph.D. program. His dad said if there was ever anything he could do for me, to let him know. I will contact him."

They spend the rest of the day studying books and websites on dolphins and whales both written from scientific and Native American perspectives. They find several online science sites that describe cetacean classification, behaviors, environments, and communities. They also happen upon several online articles about "TEK", Traditional Ecological Knowledge, a category of study popularized by Native American scientist and author Robin Wall Kimmerer[28] and others. TEK advocates say we should not assume that widely accepted theories stated in science books regarding the natural world are always right and that differing native views are wrong. This inclusion approach has led to new and productive dialogues in the field of environmental science.[29]

Nana also reads dolphin and whale stories from Native American teaching tales and Creation stories. When they discover orca grandmothers are key to the survival of their grandchildren, they all get up and do a happy dance. Nana turns her music up loud and Maddie forgets she can't dance. They all "dance until they drop."

PERMISSION AND PACKING

"Nana, how far are the San Juan Islands from here?" Maddie wonders.

"It's a two-hour drive to the ferry in Anacortes, Washington. We must arrive at least thirty minutes before departure, and the ferry takes a little over an hour to San Juan. We will need to stay over at least one night, two nights would be best."

"I don't know if Dad will give me permission. He didn't even want me to go on the school field trip. Mom and my teacher had to convince him," sighs Maddie.

"Doesn't he work where Frank works?" Nana asks.

"Yes," Maddie and Sam answer in unison.

"Let me talk to Frank and Sarah, Maddie. Stay hopeful," Nana says encouragingly. "It's time for you two to get home. It's getting dark. I'll drive you."

The next morning Nana arrives at Sam's house in time for breakfast. "What brings you here so early, Nana?" asks Frank.

"Do you work with Maddie's dad?" Nana asks.

"Yes and no," responds Frank. "We're working on different projects and have totally different leadership; however, we do see each other in the lunchroom several times a week. We sit together sometimes and mostly talk about the kids."

Nana explains why she wants to travel to the San Juan Islands with the children, and Maddie's concern about getting permission.

"Maddie's mom came into Uplift last week, and we talked briefly. I said we should have lunch sometime and she seemed agreeable. I'll invite her to the new outdoor café on Lake Loomis," added Sarah.

"Maddie says her dad's work is not going well. As a result, he is quite tense and strict with her. Perhaps her parents would appreciate a weekend alone. We just have to build trust with them. It's hard to trust when you're worried and tense," responds Nana.

After Frank leaves for work, Nana and Sam help Sarah harvest thyme and rosemary from her herb garden, which she has conveniently located right outside the kitchen door. When their baskets are full, they wash and dry the herbs thoroughly, then place them in the air dryer in the garage. After the herbs have dried, Sarah will put them in labeled bottles.

Over the next week, Frank talks with Maddie's dad several times, and her mom happily agrees to lunch with Sarah. Maddie's mom is enthusiastic about the trip and the time alone with her husband. Her husband's favorite band is playing at the Tacoma Dome in a few weeks, and she suggests those dates. Maddie's father slowly comes to trust Frank and finally agrees it would be good to have some time alone with his wife, with the possible concert as an extra bonus.

Nana contacts her friend at the CHP Institute with Maddie's parents' preferred dates. Her friend must juggle a few things to clear those dates but manages it and the trip is scheduled for a weekend slot coming up in two weeks, just before the kids return to school.

A few days before the trip, Nana sets up a three-way phone call with Maddie's and Sam's families. "Put your phones on speaker so we can all hear each other," she guides. "Let's discuss what to pack. We need food for the car and ferry ride, clothes for the weekend as well as notebooks, pens, and a camera for recording. Food first. Are you two allergic to anything?"

"No," Maddie and Sam respond in turn.

"Is there anything you don't like?" continues Nana.

"I don't like sour things like pickles," answers Maddie.

"I like my sandwiches dry, no mayo, mustard, or sauce," answers Sam.

"How about blocks of cheese, crackers, hard-boiled eggs from our chickens, and apples and berries from the garden? Bring your own filled water bottles," Nana declares.

"No cookies?" Sam laughs.

"I thought you might be tired of them," answers Nana.

"Never!" everyone answers in unison.

"What should Maddie pack?" her mother asks.

"We need to layer our clothing. We can have sun and warmth one minute and rain and hail the next. Especially now with climate chaos, we must be prepared for anything. Windbreakers with hoods are best. We can wrap them around our waists when it warms up," Nana explains.

"No problem," Maddie's mom continues, "but what about boat rides? By the way, we don't want Maddie swimming in the ocean without us there."

"Understood," soothes Nana. "A wet suit or a swimsuit with rain gear over it works for the boat."

Frank asks Maddie's dad about the concert, and they all discuss music for a few minutes before saying goodbye.

The next evening Maddie's dad comes home with a present for Maddie.

"For me?" she asks.

"Go ahead and open it," her dad says excitedly, and Maddie does.

"A wet suit! Oh, Dad, thank you so much," Maddie cries as she falls into her father's arms.

"Here, Maddie, you can have our extra cell phone with a camera. We want you to stay in touch with us, and you can take pictures to share as well."

Maddie just stares at her dad. She has asked for a phone so many times, but her parents don't want her on social media.

"No social media allowed, Maddie, but you can call and text us, use the voice and camera to record your experiences, and you can call Sam," her dad says with a huge smile on his face.

"You enjoy your weekend with Mom. I love you!" Maddie says, and they hug again for a very long time. Maddie feels like she has finally come home. Sparks joyously wags his tail nearby.

CAR AND FERRY

The morning of the trip, Nana and Sam put their luggage in the car and drive to Maddie's.

Nana is beaming with excitement about the adventure ahead. Turning to Maddie she says, "Maddie, if you don't mind, I'd like Sam in the front passenger seat. He has an amazing sense of direction. Since he was little, we've joked that he has an inner compass. No matter what the situation, he always finds a way out. I put notebooks and pens in the back in case we come up with questions for the CHP staff. Will you be our recorder?"

"Sure, I'd be glad to record. Wow, Sam, add navigating to your gift list!" Maddie comments as she puts her luggage in the trunk and climbs into the back seat.

"Here's my phone, Sam," Nana says, her voice exuding confidence. "I have the ferry terminal set as our destination on Google Maps. You're my navigator."

"You bet, Nana," exclaims Sam, "I sort of like being the captain!"

"We're giving ourselves an extra hour in case traffic is bad," Nana explains. There is an accident along the way, and they are all relieved they have the extra time. When traffic finally thins out, they start talking about the goals for the visit.

"I want to talk to the other Listeners on staff," Maddie says. "I want to know who they are talking to and what they are hearing."

"I want to see how they are scientifically tracking the migration patterns and health of the whales and dolphins—especially orcas. How do they know who's who?" Sam adds.

"I want to know how the Listeners on staff and those applying the scientific method relate to one another. What do they learn from each other's perspectives and approaches?" Nana adds.

They arrive at the ferry terminal forty-five minutes before departure.

"Wow, that's a long line of cars!" Maddie observes.

Nana explains, "Those cars are driving onto the ferry, Maddie. We don't need a car. My friend will pick us up and be our chaperone for the weekend, so I will park in the area designated for foot traffic."

Maddie gets out of the car, takes a deep breath of clean sea air, and relaxes as the waves lap rhythmically against the pier. She feels the wind on her face, hears the seagulls circling, and is content.

Sam digs a map of the ferry route out of his backpack. "Dad had this in his study and thought I would enjoy it."

They have about twenty minutes before boarding time, so they take their backpacks off. Sam sits on his suitcase and studies the map while Nana chats with the couple ahead of them in line. Maddie's awareness is opening wider and wider, until it is as open as the Salish Sea before her.

As the line starts to move, Nana gets out their tickets and says, "There are three levels on the ferry. The first is most protected from the wind and is the best place to eat. The snack shop and restrooms are on the second level, as well as more seats. The top level is standing room only, and it is cold and windy, but the view is exciting. We'll set up camp on the first, have a snack, and then you two can go exploring."

They find a booth in a protected corner on the first level. As they eat their snack, Sam asks, "Tell us about South America, Nana?"

"Like in Africa," Nana begins, "there are big modern cities, but within 50 miles, there are also Indigenous Peoples living close to the land. Once I was riding a lorry, a colorful open-air vehicle, into a new village, and when I looked at my feet, they looked like goat hooves for a moment. When we arrived in the village, I learned the people considered goats sacred. I was tuning into the energy field of the local environment. Once again, like in Africa, I experienced a different reality created by different cultural beliefs. My travels taught me how diverse human cultures are and how our beliefs form our experiences."

"Wow, Nana, you're a real adventurer!" Maddie mumbled while chewing on a sandwich.

After finishing their snack, Maddie and Sam decide to explore. "Stay close to each other and don't open up to strangers unless I am with you. Deal?" asks Nana.

"Deal!" they answer in unison.

The children explore the ferry while Nana stays with their belongings. The children find the restrooms and café where they read the menu, although they have plenty of food with Nana. Then they find the area where the cars have parked for the trip. "Yuck, too much exhaust. Let's get outta here," Sam exclaims.

"You bet!" agrees Maddie. Finally, they go up to the third level—blue water, blue sky everywhere and wind, lots of wind. "Beautiful, so beautiful," Maddie sighs.

After about an hour, they see Friday Harbor on the horizon. They go back to where Nana is seated and are docked and ready to depart thirty minutes later.

"Make sure we have everything. Let's wait until the crowd thins out a bit so we don't lose each other. Follow that exit sign," Nana advises. "My friend said he would drive the Institute van so he will be easy to spot. It's a white van with the Institute's logo on the side." They walk to the passenger pickup area.

GEORGE AND HIS HOME

"There's the white van!" exclaims Sam as it drives up to the curb. Out steps a tall, handsome man about Nana's age. He's wearing jeans, a T-shirt and cap with the Institute logo, and a windbreaker tied around his waist. Curls of white hair peek out of his cap, and his large brown eyes twinkle when he smiles. It's a sunny day and while the air is cool—especially in the shade—the sun is hot!

"So good to see you, Marjorie," he says warmly as he takes Nana's hand.

"I've never heard her called anything but Nana," thinks Maddie silently.

"Oh George, it's so good to see you too! Thanks so much for having us," Nana says warmly.

"We have the house all ready for you. My housekeeper has prepared your rooms and will make sure we're well fed!"

"I'm so sorry about your wife, George," Nana says as she puts her arm softly on his shoulder. The children notice George's tall frame shrinks. His shoulders slump, his head drops, and for an instant, grief registers on his face. Then he straightens up and is back to his charming self.

"Thanks, Marjorie," George responds as he leans gently into Nana's arm. "The children had already grown up and moved away. I miss them all." George loads the luggage in the van, and the children notice how gently he helps Nana up into the passenger seat. Nana's smile is radiant. George plays tour guide as he drives them into Friday Harbor.

"Friday Harbor is only one square mile in size and is the heart of San Juan Island," George begins. He points out the colorful shops, restaurants, bookstores, museums, and art galleries along the short route from his home.

George turns into the wooded driveway to his three-story home of western red cedar. The large house is nestled against a backdrop of Douglas fir trees. "It feels like living in a forest," Nana thinks to herself, "but there is one area cleared so his kitchen garden gets full sun." The ever-observant Nana also notices a fire pit and a picnic table in the cleared area.

George's housekeeper, Gloria, is waiting at the door as they drive up to the front entrance. She comes out to help with the luggage, and George introduces her. "Finally! Some life in this house again," she says. "Let me show you to your rooms. I've put you in a three-bedroom suite with a large balcony on the second floor."

They enter a large sitting room in the center of the suite, with three bedrooms, like spokes on a wheel around it. As they are getting settled, choosing bedrooms, and unpacking, they notice three sets of binoculars, plus lots of books and magazines on orcas, porpoises, gray whales, dolphins, terrestrial wildlife, and birds. There's also a well-attended birdfeeder and bath on the balcony.

After they unpack, they just sit in the living area amazed. After a few minutes Nana says, "I'm exhausted! I need a nap. Gloria said dinner is at 6:30. It's 5:00 now. Wake me up a little before dinner time if I don't wake up on my own."

Sam and Maddie take binoculars out to the balcony and explore as far as they can see from this vantage point, until Gloria gathers them together at 6:30.

Aromas waft through the stairwell as they approach the kitchen.

"Smells wonderful, Gloria!" exclaims Nana.

"Thanks! I made a vegetarian pasta. Are any of you vegetarian or vegan?"

"I'm not, at least not in the strictest sense," Nana answers, "although I eat mostly fruits and vegetables. I do love my chickens' eggs and cheese!" Nana answers.

"We aren't vegetarian, but we eat mostly out of our gardens. Mom is careful to avoid preservatives and additives in processed food. Nana hosts a couple of canning parties each fall, so Mom stocks up on home-canned fruits and vegetables for the winter. There's such a difference in the taste!" Sam adds.

"My folks buy food from the Fastmart on the corner store, and we aren't vegetarian, far from it!" adds Maddie.

"Good to know for future meals," Gloria says.

"You have quite a housekeeper, George," Nana comments.

"Don't call me a housekeeper!" Gloria proclaims. "If I were keeping this house, it would be organized and spotless. George has let this house go since his wife died."

George responds, "Yes, it's just too empty and lonely here. I spend most of my time at work. I did enjoy finding the books and magazines for your room, though. Maddie and Sam, Nana tells me you are in communication with the Standing Ones, the Four-legged Ones, and Winged Ones. We have staff who can communicate with the Finned Ones as well."

When the children looked surprised, he adds, "Yes, we use the indigenous names for trees, animals, birds, fish, and cetaceans, as well as the scientific names. We Western scientists are learning a lot from what we call TEK, or Traditional Ecological Knowledge. For instance, the Puyallup tribe was communicating with orcas long before the white man came to this land. They still do. During last year's ceremony, an orca swam up to their canoe and stayed there, close enough to touch."

Maddie says, "We just read about TEK and the current dialogues happening between environmental scientists, traditional elders, and wisdom keepers. I think this is cool."

George answers, "Perhaps you two will join the new breed of scientists that are emerging now. I know your gifts are rare among your families and classmates, but these gifts are returning now, amongst all earth's tribes. Have you heard of the Galactic Guardians?"

The children answer yes and share about SilverLight's teachings.

"What are your questions for this weekend?" George asks, and Maddie reads the questions she had recorded. "Good.

These are excellent! We scientists are only as good as our questions."

After dinner, Maddie and Sam go upstairs to get the binoculars, then go outside to explore. When the sky is darkened and they are looking up at the star-filled sky, SilverLight appears to their inner eyes, "I want to show you something," she says and, all of a sudden, there are no trees, no grass, no house, no stars, only points of light connected by shimmering light filaments. There are a multitude of them, all interweaving.

Cosmic Web

"Oh, SilverLight," Maddie cries out, "This is SO beautiful!"

"What is this?" Sam wonders, awestruck.

"These are the energetic grids that hold your planet together," exclaims SilverLight. "There is a grid for Mother Earth, for the trees, for each species of animal on land, sea, and air, including humans. Each point of light is a created being and the streams of light you see connect them all in an energetic network. This is how Mother Tree and Dortha know Maple. All trees are connected. All humans are connected too. When humans choose to live in harmony with nature, light-filled, healthy energy is infused into the collective grid. The opposite is true as well. The dolphins, whales, and trees know we are all connected in a circle of life. Only humans separate themselves, and this separation causes so much suffering. When humans disconnect from nature, they are disconnecting from themselves, and they forget their responsibility to be the tentative stewards of this beautiful planet."

Maddie frowns, "What do you mean 'tentative stewards?' Do we have to camp out in tents in order to be good stewards?"

SilverLight answers as she shakes her head sadly. "Tentative means 'not fixed, not certain, i.e., provisional.' While some believe humans have been ordained by the universe to be the permanent and irrevocable guardians of all life forms on earth, to have dominion over all, most of those who believe such things are humans, and may be biased. Some dragons, however, feel that the human position, even as 'stewards' or guardians of the earth, is quite tenuous, and remains to be justified. Have humans earned this right? They treat Mother Earth as a resource to be plundered, instead of a living being with which we are intimately connected. The disastrous consequences are visible for all to see. If humans are to continue living here, they must reconnect with their earthly Mother, Mother Earth: otherwise, who knows?"

The young people stand speechless, slowly absorbing the gravity of SilverLight's words. After a while SilverLight says, "Go to bed now, my friends. May your dreams be filled with the awe and wonder of this beautiful planet you live upon, and may they inspire you to be its worthy Protectors!"

"Oh, thank you for coming into our lives, SilverLight," Maddie whispers.

"Yes, we love you," murmurs Sam, and they go up to bed.

Nana and George talk into the wee hours of the night, with only a brief interruption to say good night to the young ones.

"How did you meet your husband Mark, Marjorie?" wonders George.

"I was thirty-four and had just returned from South America. We met at a friend's home and spent the night talking. He grew up on a farm that had been in his family for five generations, and he knew how to listen to the land. He was close friends with Native Americans in the area and learned from their traditional knowledge as well. His family had always rotated and diversified crops. He said, 'Love the land and it will love you back.' When his neighbors, who had chosen to grow one cash crop, found their soils deteriorating and their crops failing, they consulted Mark.

"What I had learned from my travels and what Mark learned from the land seemed to go together. We both experienced nature's sentience, its ability to perceive and feel, and we both understood our cultural stories shape our experiences.

"We were married within the year. Two years, later Sarah was born. We worked the farm and created an educational center for regenerative agriculture until we turned fifty-five and handed the farm over to Mark's younger brother. We moved to town, and you know the rest. We both understood we don't have to accept the cultural story we are given if it does not serve us well. Mark and I agreed when we got married that, to the extent the outer world would allow, we would create the story together we wanted to live." After reminiscing late into the night, George walks Marjorie to her suite and, with a kiss on the cheek, says good night.

When they return to the kitchen the next morning, pancakes and scrambled eggs are waiting.

"Yum, is this bread I smell baking?" exclaims Nana.

"I made sourdough from George's family's starter," Gloria says, "He gave it to me to keep alive when his wife died. His children can't commit to keeping it going at this time in their lives, so I'm doing what I can. I've made a sandwich bar on the counter by the window for you to make your own lunches."

"Oh, I just remembered, Sam. Go upstairs and bring me the gifts I brought for George and Gloria," Nana says. Sam brings back a box with canned fruits, vegetables, and jams inside. They open the raspberry jam to put on their pancakes.

"Where shall we start?" begins George. "Sam, you asked how we track the orca's migration patterns and how we know who's who. We'll start there, and I suspect Maddie and Nana's questions will be answered before the day is out. Now finish your breakfast and make your lunch. The Institute is just a few miles from here by boat, but much further by land. Since I don't have a seaplane, we'll have to go by car."

"I found it on the map yesterday," beams Sam, "so I know what you mean. Too far to swim there!"

"Wear your wetsuits under your clothes. We'll be spending some time on a research vessel today," advises George.

"I'll meet you at the van," Nana adds.

They have binoculars around their necks when they join Nana and George at the van.

VESSELS

As George drives them to the Cetacean Human Partnership Institute, he describes its research vessels.

"We have four vessels. OrcaLove is our largest at 140 feet. It can travel both in Puget Sound and beyond. It has room for fourteen for day trips and can sleep eight. The research lab is stellar.

"CleanWaters is our 44-foot research vessel. It stays in the Salish Sea around the San Juan Islands. It can take ten people on day trips and sleep five overnight.

We also have a smaller boat named Kaalin that takes us from one research location to another.[30]

"The other one is a catamaran, a yacht with two hulls, but one sail or one motor. The way it's built allows us to get up close to the whales for observation and, at the same time, protects us from the waves.

"All the vessels in Puget Sound are aware of our research. When a whale watching boat, for instance, spots an orca pod, they radio the location to us. We always have several boats equipped and ready, so we stop what we are doing in the Center and immediately go to the given location.

"Today, we will tour the Center and see how the individual orcas are identified and recorded. If we get a call that a pod has been sighted, we'll go out to meet it together. Did you bring cameras?"

"In my phone, yes," Maddie, Sam, and Nana each respond.

"We have waterproof pouches for your phones. Remind me to get each of you one," George adds attentively as he turns into the Center driveway and parks.

THE INSTITUTE

George wastes no time and begins the orientation lecture. "In the Salish Sea, we've got a variety of cetaceans including resident orcas, transient orcas, porpoises, and seasonal visits from minke, gray, and humpback whales."

"George, how long have you worked in cetacean research?" Nana asks as they continue walking towards the entrance.

"Since I started fishing with my grandfather in these waters as a child," George replies. "My parents and I lived in Seattle, but I spent many summers with my grandparents. Granddad told me cetaceans were special beings, part mammal, part fish, part something else we humans don't understand. He said that they were a more advanced family of species than the one we belong to, one that may have lived upon the land millions of years before us, and super intelligent. I wanted to be among the first to understand cetaceans: whales, porpoises, and dolphins. The books I read only went so far. Then I discovered that the local Native American fishermen had been carefully observing cetaceans for generations, and could answer my questions better than the textbooks, at least some of the time. I was exhilarated when the orcas breached. I felt like they were rising and breaking through the surface of the water just for me. I read and watched everything I could get my hands on about orcas and wrote many a school research paper on the subject. I had a chance to attend a summer camp here my junior year of high school, and the next summer, I was hired on as staff. I got my Ph.D. from the University of Washington in the Marine Biology Department and did my dissertation research here."[31]

A huge wooden sculpture of an orca hangs above the entrance. As they walk inside the main lobby, they see lots of large, framed photographs of cetaceans. Each is labeled with its scientific and common name. The orca labels also include a letter and number.

"What do those letters and numbers mean?" asks Maddie.

"The letter identifies the pod, and the number shows the order in which the individual was identified," explains George. "I'll explain in more detail when we go into the computer lab. This picture," he continues pointing to a large portrait, "is of Dr. Michael Bigg, the founder of modern whale research.[32] His work was with the transient orcas who have a wider migratory pattern and a different diet from the resident orcas. These two groups don't mix, even when they are relatively close to one another. Bigg realized that the saddle patches on orcas are distinctive, like our fingerprints, and that, along with unique fin characteristics, can be used to identify individuals. Some scientists mocked him at first.[33]

"Dr. Bigg is in good company. The men who first discovered the earth is round, not flat, were persecuted, as were those that realized it revolves around the sun. Louis Pasteur met violent resistance when he put forward the idea that germs cause illness. Today, those of us who understand all life is sentient are often derided by those who don't. It takes courage to be a pioneer."

Sam says, "Now I know what sentient means: the ability to perceive and feel. I believe all life is sentient too!"

"Let me give you the grand tour," George continues with a twinkle in his eye, as he leads them through the building. The harbor views from the large picture windows are breathtaking. He shows them the locker room where they can store anything they don't want to carry, the lunchroom, and the restrooms. There is a large equipment room housing drones and nautical equipment, plus conference rooms and study carrels. "Here," George says as he opens a large double doorway, "is the computer lab!"

ORCA HEAVEN

Wall-to-wall computers and monitors fill the lab. George leads them to one monitor, and says, "This is the resident orca identification catalogue. Dr. Bigg died in 1990, but his research has continued both here and in Canada with both the transient and resident populations. No whales have been studied more. We start photographing the calves as soon as possible and photograph them annually since the saddle patches grow as the whales grow, and the fins can develop distinguishing shapes and nicks too. Before digital cameras, we had to spend our nights developing film. The first year, we took about 17,000 photos. Now with digital cameras we shoot 200,000 to 300,000 per year.[34]

"Resident orca society is matriarchal, and all offspring stay with the mother and grandmother for life. However, transient orca males often leave their mothers and go off on their own. Transient orca daughters stay with their mothers and grandmothers. Even after the matriarch dies, these matrilineal bonds remain tight. A group of matrilines who play, feed, and travel together is called a pod.[35] Members of the pod are never more than a few miles apart, and they communicate through underwater vocalizations."[36]

George introduces a technician seated nearby. "Sam, Maddie, and Marjorie, this is Thomas," and one-by-one they shake hands. "Give your phones to Thomas and he'll put a link to our ID database on them so you can upload your photos to our system."

"If you show me how, I can do it myself," Maddie says. Sam agrees, and Thomas shows them both how.

ORCA SIGHTING

Suddenly, the sound of chimes fills the lab. "A pod has been located! Let's go!" George announces.

As they leave the computer room, Nana reminds George of the waterproof camera pouches. George stops at the equipment room and gives each of them a waterproof parka, life jacket, and pouch. Maddie, Sam, and Nana all have George's binoculars around their necks as well.

"You're wearing your wetsuits, aren't you?" he asks. "Good," he continues as they nod yes. "Put your other clothes in your locker, and meet me at the back door."

In the locker room, Maddie takes the hollow gull bone out of her jacket and puts it in the pocket of her waterproof parka as more chimes signal a second sighting. They all hurry to meet George at the back door.

"We'll take CleanWaters," George says as he opens the back door and guides them to the dock. "Our small drone can be flown from it, and we might get some good film from the two different sightings."

As they board the vessel along with research staff and crew, Maddie sees a picture of a mother and baby orca in her mind's eye. Her hand instinctively goes to her hollow gull bone in her windbreaker's pocket, and she's filled with warm, motherly love.

"Maddie, this is Susan WindSong. She's our staff oceanographer and she's of Native American descent. Her people have traditionally lived closely with orcas and see them as their spiritual relatives. They call orcas 'the people who live under the sea,'" George says.

"Yes, Maddie, our Puyallup elders believe all whales have an important role to play in keeping the ecosystem healthy. Western beliefs have seen them as resources to exploit, and we are all suffering as a result," Susan says sadly.

"Susan, Maddie is a Listener. You two go up to the view deck just above the bridge," George suggests as he points to the stairs. "You'll have the broadest view. There's a cushioned bench if you need to sit."

"I've got George's binoculars!" exclaims Maddie.

"You can use the radio up there if needed. Just remember that anything you say into the radio will be broadcast on a loudspeaker throughout the boat," warns George.

Maddie and Susan climb the stairs to the small observation deck and sit on the cushioned benches where they have an unobstructed view of the sea. Susan notices Maddie is holding a bone. "What's in your hand, Maddie?"

"My hollow gull bone. It's a gift to remind me to stay open and listen."

Susan reaches into her shirt and pulls a bone out of her medicine pouch. "This is my hollow eagle bone. It reminds me to stay open to spirit. Do you know why bird bones are hollow?"

"Is it to make them lighter?" Maddie asks.

"Not exactly. It's because their lungs actually extend into their bones! While the bones are hollow inside, the outside of the bones are very strong and are just as heavy as the bones of other animals. The hollow cavities allow more airflow to and from the lungs, and with the extra strong outer bone, the birds' stamina is increased for long flights," Susan says as she studies Maddie carefully.[37]

"Maddie, what have you seen?"

"I felt a Mother Orca with her baby," Maddie responds.

"Ahhh, a message. Let's stay quiet and see what she can teach us."

Meanwhile, Sam is drawn to the drone on deck. Several technicians are preparing it for flight, and George asks the technicians to explain the process to Sam.

"This is our Phantom 4 Pro V2 drone. It's small enough to launch from this boat. Metal can interfere with its compass, so we use this spot to set up and launch. We do have to catch it by hand upon return, and the catcher wears extensive safety gear," explains one of the technicians.

"Do the drones bother the orcas?" Sam asks.

"Not that we are aware of, no. They continue with their normal activities," the technician continues.

"How much footage can you film in one outing?" asks Sam.

"We can get between one and two hours on an average day."

"Can you see what you are filming in real time?"

"Yes, sometimes. We have a monitor, but we can't see the details until we view the footage on a large screen."

"How close can you get to the orcas?"

"Once launched, we motor parallel to the whales, usually from 200 to 400 feet away."

"What have you learned from the drone footage?"

"Orcas are very social creatures, lots of social touch and interaction, even when it appears they are resting."[38]

While Sam is learning the mechanics of the drone, Maddie and Susan are making contact with the orcas.

"They are coming closer," Maddie reports.

"What do you feel, Maddie?" Susan asks.

"I feel the mother's love and delight. It's so strong and beautiful. The child is full of joy and playfulness."

"I feel them approaching. I'll tell the captain to turn off the motors," Susan whispers.

Susan turns on the radio and announces, "Mother and child approaching. Code Quiet."

"What's Code Quiet?" whispers Maddie.

"It signals the crew to turn off the motors and all on board to quiet, wait, hold space, and listen."

Within ten minutes, the new mother from J pod and her healthy baby are swimming alongside the boat within Maddie and Susan's view.

"Do you want to go down closer, Maddie?"

"No, I feel like I am with them. I couldn't get any closer. I'm also getting flashes about noise, junk in the water, and feelings of hunger, but all within a sense of deep peace. Hmmm."

"Yes," Susan says, "will share more later. I'm feeling that she came to meet you, Maddie. Just stay connected now."

The only sounds on the boat are the wind, the waves, and the click of digital cameras. The mother and child stay within view for twenty minutes. When they swim away, Susan announces on the radio, "Follow them. They will lead you to her pod. They are feeding." When they reach the pod, they are indeed feeding, and the drone is launched twice. The research staff is excited about the footage.

Maddie and Sam lean over the railing to get a closer look at an adolescent whale that is swimming alongside the boat. Maddie gazes into one eye of the whale. She calls out, in a

KAALIN

KAALIN IS THE QUINAULT TRIBE'S WORD FOR ORCA.

sing-song voice as if to a puppy, "... and what's YOUR name?"

The eye of the whale seems to sparkle for a moment, and then the whale thrusts its flipper up through the water, sending a well-aimed jet of cold water right at Maddie. Maddie is soon soaked. "What the heck was that for???" she squeals. Sam and George are standing right beside her but are dry as a bone, thanks to the whale's remarkable aim. George is doubled over in laughter, chuckling so hard he can hardly breathe.

"You asked her what her name was, Maddie!"

"Yeah, so? What's her name?"

"We all call her 'Splasher!' Did you see this black mark on her dorsal fin? This's how we know it's her, and that's what we call her, and this's what she likes to do. She just answered your question. Looks like you just had an interspecies experience!"

Maddie's eyes are like saucers. "I just talked to a whale and a whale answered?"

"Yup! Let me get you a towel," George adds. "You don't want to get cold!"

As Maddie is drying off, they hear several crew members yell, "Help needed!" from the other side of the boat. They turn, hurry over, and spot an orca entangled in commercial fishing lines. The orca has come for help. George and several crew members put on their scuba gear and dive in. Sam and Maddie see a faint silver mist surrounding the orca and the divers. "SilverLight," whispers Maddie as she spontaneously reaches out for Sam's hand. It takes several hours and careful maneuvering to free the orca. It's dangerous work. One thrash of a tail can kill a diver. However, the orca has come for help and remains as still as possible. After the orca is freed and the divers are back on board, the orca swims up to the boat. He comes up to each diver individually and stares eye to eye before swimming off. The three divers stand transfixed. "This was the most incredible experience of my life," one of the divers says, and the others nod in agreement, lost for words.

It is late afternoon when they return to the Institute with film to upload and experiences to discuss. Everyone is especially excited about the photos of the new baby, who is added to the J pod matriline.

"Susan, would you join us for dinner? I'm sure our guests have questions, and it would be good to have a more intimate setting for our conversation," asks George.

Susan laughs, "Oh, I'd accept just for Gloria's cooking, let alone the company!"

Sam wants to hear all about Maddie's experience, but George suggests they wait until dinner.

AN UNEXPECTED DINNER GUEST

Gloria makes a lentil meatloaf that everyone loves. Susan asks for the recipe, and Gloria goes into the study to make a copy

"Ok, Maddie and Susan, we want to hear everything," begins George. "Maddie, what is it like to communicate with whales?"

"I felt so expansive, like we were as wide as the ocean together. I've never felt such a deep sense of calm. Even when she sent me flashes of noise, pollution, and hunger, I felt no anger or fear from her.[39] She was so delighted with her calf and her calf was a bundle of joy! Mother's love was so profound it seemed to fill the ocean," Maddie shares. A deep quiet settles over the dinner table. Gloria tiptoes back into the room with the recipe, and tears fall down Nana's cheeks.

"Mother and calf are with us now. They are joining us through Maddie. Thank you, Maddie, thank you beloved orcas," Susan says. "The Indigenous Peoples of the Pacific Northwest have always communicated telepathically with cetaceans, including my people, the Puyallup. It was, and still is to some degree, a part of our culture. We know how gentle, kind, and wise they are. They teach us to be in the present moment and follow the natural flow of life. They are vital to the health of our oceans, and our oceans are vital to the health of the earth."

George clears his throat and speaks in a low tone, conveying a feeling of deep seriousness. He says, "The oceans are warming as well as rising, due to climate change, and whales will have to adapt to or migrate away from warmer waters. NOAA predicted that the oceans along the coasts of the United States will rise one foot by 2050, 7 ½ feet by 2100, and 13 feet by 2150."[40]

"Noah said that? The guy with the ark?" Maddie says with her eyes wide and jaw slackened. "Well I guess he'd know about predicting great floods, wouldn't he? I mean, is that a biblical prophecy? Or a Native American one? I heard that the Hopi, too, predicted that oceans would rise . . ."

"Oh, no, sorry. That's N-O-A-A The National Oceanic and Atmospheric Administration, in Washington, D.C. Even the Pentagon is concerned because every foot the ocean rises we'll lose

100 feet of shoreline, and everyone there will have to move."

Everyone is silent until Gloria brings out dessert. Nana wants to know how the indigenous and scientific perspectives work together. George and Susan explain that the TEK movement is a work in progress; the two belief systems are opposites in some ways. Indigenous People are close to the land. They watch what the plants and animals do and learn from them. It's a personal and reciprocal relationship with all of life. Science strives to be objective through systematic observation, measurement, and testing.

"Telepathic communication," Susan says, "cannot be observed, measured, or tested with our five senses. Science is crucial to learning about orcas, but it is just beginning to understand all life is sentient and that we need the whales' perspective, too, if we want to survive together on this planet. There are many roads to knowledge, and science is certainly one of them, but human knowledge is in its infancy compared to cetacean knowledge. However, there is a bridge, and some call it telepathy, but sometimes it is more like television!"

Maddie responds, "Yes, I think I've tuned into their station lately. But how do I know what's true and what's imagination?"

Susan answers, "Trust in the *possibility* of interspecies telepathic communication, but then do your best to *verify*. This is why I like this place. We verify stuff! What I have learned here, using human science, has helped me verify at least half of my visions; the other half will be verified sooner or later, maybe in a few hundred years. Meanwhile, I know what I know."

As the evening is winding down, George brings out a book to share. "I highly recommend this book by Mary J. Getten,

Communicating with Orcas: The Whales' Perspective. I want to read a paragraph from it. This is a message from Granny, the matriarch of J Pod. She gave it telepathically to Raphaela, an animal communicator who worked with Mary.

'*Know and understand your connections and mutual dependence on our planet. Love it. Protect it. Your existence depends on it. You are children of the beloved earth, sky, wind, and water. When you detach, you die. There is a wave of changing consciousness on the planet. It is part of our mission to foster it by sharing our presence with you.*'"[41]

"Maddie, Sam, and Nana, I would like to stay in touch with you," Susan says as she gets up to leave.

"I was thinking about asking Chief Calming Thunder to spend some time with us as well. We want to learn from the indigenous perspective," Nana adds.

"I know Phillip," Susan says, "I'll call him too."

"I'd like to come visit you too," George says while smiling lovingly at Nana, and Nana blushes.

"You all have an open invitation to my home. I have extra bedrooms, and you can stay as long as you like. Talk to Phillip and send me some possible dates. Hopefully we can have regular mentoring sessions. Phillip has lots to share about leadership, and Susan is an experienced Listener."

They continue to feel Mother Orca's presence as they are saying good-bye. After lots of long hugs, Susan leaves with a goodie bag of dinner leftovers. Everyone else helps Gloria clean up, and they agree it will be a sad moment when it's time to catch the ferry tomorrow and go back to school. Sam and Maddie go upstairs to bed with full hearts.

DREAMTIME SAM

Sam is so exhausted he tumbles into bed without changing into his pajamas and falls instantly asleep. He finds himself at the Mother Tree. Owl is speaking with him and SilverLight is present. "Have you discovered the promise you made to Creator yet?" asks Owl.

"No, I have no idea what happened before I was born, but I know my mission here and now. I am an apprentice to the Galactic Guardians, and I am willing to learn. I am to live my life in a way that brings in the new world."

"Same thing," says Owl wryly as he winks. "Nana the Elder has owl medicine. Her wisdom is deep. She is surrendered to Creator and will support and guide you. Stay close to her."

"I will," Sam responds.

"I have excellent hearing, you know," Owl says, "and I can hear the slightest sound, and I will hear you when you call. But Maddie here is the best listener! Open your heart and tell her how you feel, Sam. She is your 'owl'—your wild bird, the one that flies free but will come when you call, to tell you what she has heard. Trust her with your secrets—the good news and the bad—and she will support you. She has your back."

"I am here for you as well," says Mother Tree, as streams of sparkling green light move up from her roots, lighting her trunk and soaring into the cosmos. Streams of crystalline light flow down from the cosmos into her leaves, trunk, roots, and soil. "I am here for you as well," says SilverLight as the green and crystalline energies surround them and bind them together—young man, Mother Tree, dragon, and owl.

Suddenly SilverLight becomes very solid in the lush green landscape of Sam's dream. Her face seems to grin from ear to ear with a glow of excitement. She rears up and flings a soccer ball at Sam and cries out, "Heads up!!"

"What?" Sam yells back as the ball bounces off his head and back into SilverLight's hands.

"Game tomorrow! No time to goof off. Remember what I told you!" SilverLight flings the ball again at Sam.

"Hey, there's no game tomorrow! What are you talking about?" Sam stops the ball with his knee.

BEND IT LIKE BUDDHA!

Suddenly the dreamscape clouds up and changes. When the clouds fade, Sam finds himself standing in a soccer stadium in the midst of a championship game. Owl and Mother Tree have shape-shifted into human players. Sam runs the ball toward a distant goal, but SilverLight stands in his way downfield, rearing up and literally standing on the tips of her big-clawed toes.

"What?" he yells out.

He runs the ball to the left to avoid SilverLight, but she, too, moves to the left as if to block his path. Now his heart races. He starts to panic. He thinks, "I am no match for a dragon! It's not fair! SilverLight, aren't you going to help me score this goal? Come on!"

"But I AM helping! I am helping to challenge you to play on a higher level of skill! This goal means nothing. What's important is reaching your goals in life. Soccer is your particular way of working out your life's problems in real time!"

"Wow, really?? Do I do this? Yeah, maybe I do, I don't know. But right now, you are in my way . . ."

"The way that can be spoken of is not the way."

"What? But you are in MY WAY!! That's what I'm talking about!"

"Yes, the way of truth, the Beauty Way, the way of the eternal, the way of Tao, the way of . . . well you get the idea. This is just a dress rehearsal!"

SilverLight runs right up to Sam, blocking his way with her huge frame. He tries to pass the ball forward to Owl, but SilverLight blocks it with her long leg and kicks it back to him. He moves yet further left, but then the ball spurts away toward the foul line. Suddenly it seems like the dream is passing in slow motion. Sam thinks, "If I kick the ball out of bounds, the other team gets the throw-in and I lose possession. If I lose possession, I lose the game. And then I'll never be captain!"

SilverLight says, "Lose possession? I heard your thoughts! You are reacting out of fear, not playfulness. You are losing possession of love, my friend! Remember to be playful. Love what you're doing, win or lose, and you will be great!"

"Look, you already are captain!" SilverLight continued. "You've always been captain of this ship! This field is the landscape of your soul. Believe in yourself."

Sam looks down to his left arm and sees a golden armband tied around it. There is a red stripe on it and the image of a golden dragon on it. It is his badge as captain. He is so happy he leaps into the air, lands ahead of the ball, and gives that spheroid a masterful heel kick just before it goes out of play. It sails back to SilverLight, who stops the ball under her right foot and stands there as if to challenge Sam further.

Her eyes are flashing with bolts of blue electricity. Smoke is shooting out of her large nostrils. She kicks the ball with great force at Sam and says, "See, dragons can play soccer too!"

"That's what I was afraid of!" Sam shudders as he kicks the ball back.

"You have NOTHING to fear, Sam. You and I have mind-melded. We are in the ONENESS! You can do ANYTHING I can!"

Sam, breathless, says, "You *gotta* be kidding!"

"No kidding. I CHALLENGE you. You've been practicing your footwork? Show me what you GOT!"

Sam kicks the ball towards SilverLight as hard as he can, but the dragon stretches out her huge tail as fast as lightning and knocks the ball back with the same velocity. Now Sam is sorry he kicked so hard as now when the two confront each other the ball ricochets back and forth between them like a pinball out of control.

Sam thinks, "Pinball! I used to play a mean pinball! I can do this!" He looks up to the stadium scoreboard, but it's now a pinball scoreboard. There is a game clock that says 85:00, five minutes left to play. Every time either player kicks the ball, the scoreboard dings and the score advances ten points, more like pinball than the slow scoring of soccer. Ding ding ding ding, the kicking grows faster.

"Show me what you're made of, Sam!" the dragon calls.

Sam elevates the ball to try and kick it over the dragon's head, but SilverLight just rears and butts it off her head, bouncing it back to Sam's head, and the two start heading it back and forth at blinding speed, as if in some kind of non-verbal conversation.

With a toss of his head, Sam elevates again, but SilverLight spreads her wings and begins to rise up in the air. She heads the ball back again. Sam punts it to the side, but SilverLight is there in a flash, still in the air, and sends it back. Sam jumps high to bunt it with his knees but keeps flying. He stays up in the air.

Hummingbird appears at the edge of Sam's vision, saying, "Come on, Sam! Learn to adapt! You can do it!" Sam starts darting from side to side, deflecting one volley after another, as SilverLight begins to shoot more and more difficult kicks at him.

"Not bad, kid! Now you're thinking like an Air dragon! But there's a bigger game after this. It's called life. I hope you can take the heat!"

SilverLight begins to breathe fire, careful not to singe Sam, but instinctively Sam belches back a cloud of smoke and mist at SilverLight. She calls, "You are a Fire dragon now. Good for you! But this is just part of who you really are. Now it's time to ground your energies and come down to earth. Time to learn teamsmanship!"

SilverLight drifts down to earth. Now there are eleven dragons on the field, all wearing silver tunics and ready to defend their goal zone. She is one of them.

Sam, too, drifts back down to the ground, and tries to run the ball past them all, but the clock shows 88 minutes, only two minutes left. Sam declares, "I am a team player, not a one-man show! No one can win a championship alone. Where are MY dragons?"

Ten dragons appear, wearing the same yellow uniform.

"Who are you?" Sam calls.

"We are the Master Dragons, masters of earth, water, fire, and air. We are here to help you reach your goal." The speed of the relays between them is staggering, and they keep one step ahead of SilverLight's incredible team of players, their tails lashing wildly as they play. The crowd roars in excitement. "Olé! Olé!"

Sam approaches the penalty box before the opponents' net and posts, only to find SilverLight herself as goal tender, seeming very relaxed, picking her teeth with a silver wishbone. She says, "Your wish is my command, Sam. Don't delay. The planet is running out of time! Finish what you started, for the benefit of all sentient beings! Bend it like Buddha! Just do it!"

A dragon knocks the ball in front of Sam. He tees it up with his instep and curls it to the side of SilverLight, a perfect swerve kick. She falls on the ball, but it goes through into the net for the winning point. She lies there for a moment, then turns her head towards Sam and winks one eye.

The dream changes again, and suddenly, the pinball scoreboard has only one team listed. It says WORLD CUP and there is only one score. The score is "one." The clock hits 90 minutes, and a deafening buzzer echoes throughout the world stadium. Sam awakens with a jolt and sits up in bed, staring at a large digital bedside clock, provided by the Cetacean Institute. The panels drop down with a soft click—1:00 A.M. His heart is racing. He arrives in the waking state as one coming back from a long journey. "What a doozie that was! And I thought I was going to dream about whales and dolphins tonight!"

He picks up his cell phone to check the time. The phone battery is dead, and he realizes it has not made a sound the entire weekend. Before bed, he was worried about getting up at six A.M. for the ride home, but now he wonders how he'll get back to sleep so he can wake up at six, when the real-world buzzer will go off.

DREAMTIME MADDIE

Maddie puts on her pajamas and packs up for the trip home. She makes sure her hollow gull bone is protected. She has quite a sunburn and feels her face burning as she falls asleep and begins to dream.

She finds herself in a desert with her family. They are dehydrated, weak, and close to death. Maddie clutches her hollow gull bone and weakly prays, "Help." Suddenly a cloud in the shape of Splasher appears overhead, and it starts to rain. Maddie and her family are soon soaked and cooled. The rain turns into a major downpour, and all they have to do is hold their canteens up to the sky and they are filled with water. "Thank you, Splasher," Maddie says with great relief.

Next, she is sitting against Dortha, the Douglas fir tree. Squirrel and Chipmunk are at her feet and Hummingbird is hovering in front of her eyes. Looking up she notices a bright star shining above Dortha. She gazes at it for a moment then says to herself, "Starlight, star bright, first star I see tonight, I wish I may, I wish I might, never forget how I feel tonight."

"You don't give up, even when life is difficult. You have strong squirrel medicine, Maddie. So does Nana the Elder;

she's great at putting food away for winter! Stay close to her," Squirrel declares.

"I will," responds Maddie.

"Maddie the Listener, we hummingbirds are capable of amazing feats and so are you! We are small, but very adaptable. We can fly long distances and even fly backwards! You can hear us while many humans are still deaf to our wisdom and gifts. Spread our messages!"

"How can I do this, Hummingbird?"

"Stay light and joyful. Play! Hum your own song even when those around you are grumbling. Creator will guide you."

"Follow your inspiration!" adds Chipmunk. "Be spontaneous, ever light on your feet; when one branch ends, jump to another one."[42].

As Maddie relaxes against Dortha, she feels sparkling green energy coming up from Dortha's roots, into her trunk, leaves, and into the cosmos and crystalline light coming down from the cosmos, filling and weaving her, Dortha, Hummingbird, Chipmunk, and Squirrel together.

NANA SLEEPS

After Gloria has gone home, Nana and George sit quietly together in the living room, sharing stories of the past and hopes for the future. Nana is tired, but deeply satisfied when she finally climbs the stairs and prepares for bed. She falls asleep quickly and dreams.

She is sitting in a circle with Mother Tree and SilverLight. There is a hummingbird flying above their heads, a chipmunk at their feet, and an owl and squirrel looking down from a nearby tree.

"Nana the Elder, stay close to our young apprentices. They hold the future. Guide them with your wisdom," Mother Tree advises.

"I will," Nana promises as a golden light fills the circle.

COMING HOME

Sam can't quite believe he will have to go back to school in just a few hours. The early morning drive homeward is a pleasant one; however, at first dark and quiet, then painted in sunrise colors. A single bright star crowns the flamboyant eastern sky. It is the morning star, shining like a diamond. Sam keeps his eyes fixed upon it. "When you wish upon a star, your dreams come true. Who said this? Jiminy Cricket? Or some indigenous elder 10,000 years ago? I wish that I never forget how I feel right now. Ever!"

Frank and Sarah ask Nana, Sam, and Maddie to come into the backyard. Sitting on their back fence is an owl with white, silver, and gold feathers and a heart-shaped face. Its dark eyes pierce a message through Sam's mind, "I am always watching and listening!" Maddie hears it, too, and she and Sam stand looking at each other, knowingly.

Frank holds up his cell phone and says, "Son, did you check

your phone for messages? I've been calling you all weekend, every few hours!"

"Oh, sorry, Dad. The battery died, and I was so busy learning about whales that I forgot all about it! I guess I thought that nothing was more important than saving the planet."

"Well, don't overdo it. You might miss some steps along the way. Apparently, you had a rainout game two weeks ago and it was rescheduled for today on short notice!"

"Really? That was a big game! Against our division rivals!"

"Yes, and you have permission from the principal to leave class early to warm up. Best of luck!" Frank's cell phone rings with the sound of African marimbas playing a lively tune. He takes the call. The marimbas stop. His eyebrows lift up higher than Sam has ever seen as he listens intently. He is quiet for a long time. All are holding their breath. What could it be?

Finally, Frank says, "Do you want to speak to him? He's right here!" Frank pauses then speaks again. All are staring at the phone. "Yes, he's finally back. No? You don't want to speak to him? Okay, five minutes. We'll be out front!"

Frank clicks the phone off. He takes a breath. "Okay, that was your head coach, Doc Hadley, the hard-headed old bird you are always telling me about. He'll be arriving in five minutes. He has something to ask you, some kind of favor. Sounds like you should stick around for this."

"Gulp! Uh, sure. I'll wait." They go to the front of the house. Sam paces nervously for five minutes. In exactly five minutes, the head coach's car pulls up. He steps out and shakes everyone's hand. He seems a little nervous.

"Sam, I'm really worried about the game this afternoon. Our

senior player, you know Fast Fernando Diaz, is in the hospital with a high fever and a choking cough. It might be COVID. They don't know. The other players are good but they are not, well, it's hard to get them to think like a team. They need someone to keep their heads in the game, to keep them focused, a team leader. I got the phone call about Fernando on Sunday and started to get worried. Then that night, last night, I had a dream that you were this knight wielding a lance, and you were riding on the back of a golden dragon, and you led us to victory. Is that crazy, or what? But I follow hunches, as a lot of coaches do but won't admit. I'm going to ask you a favor. Can you wear this in today's game?"

Doc Hadley pulls a yellow armband out of the breast pocket of his sports coat and dusts it off. It is some kind of yellow bandana tied together in a knot. He holds it out, but does not give it to Sam. "Sam, I warn you, it's not an actual captain's golden armband. There's a lot of red tape, and all these votes you have to get to become captain in a varsity game, and we just don't have time. But I came up with this."

Sam is speechless, and maintains a poker face, not daring to touch it.

"This isn't some kind of . . ."

"No, it's no joke, Sam. I'll do anything to win this game. The whole school needs you to help us save this win. I'll even bet on a crazy dream that you can help save our skin. Can you do it?"

Sam answers, "A golden dragon? That is a crazy dream, coach. You sure it wasn't silver? But in any case, I'll do whatever it takes to lead us to victory. Thanks for believing in me and the dream. I'll wear this bandana, armband, whatever."

"I know it's not a real one, Sam. This morning when I woke up,

I wanted to ignore the dream. I thought it was too crazy. But I told my wife the dream, and she said, 'Give the kid a chance, Paul.'

"At first, I said, 'No!' But then she gave me this look, like, 'Better think twice about this Paul!' She's from Canada. We met over in Vancouver, but she's originally from the province of New Brunswick, and a proud fan of the Fredericton Junior Red Wings. Well, that's hockey, but she is also a fan of the Fredericton Regional District Junior Men's Soccer League and donates each year. So, she marches into the living room and comes back with a 9 x 12 inch replica of the New Brunswick flag on a post and plops it down in front of me. I know it's very special to her, and I look at it, and I see there is this golden dragon on a red stripe floating across the top of the flag against a golden field. She says, 'Let the kid take captain! What have you got to lose?' Then she rips the yellow-colored flag from the pole and says, 'Let him wear this as his armband!'"

Coach Hadley unties the cloth and shows Sam it is the flag of the province of New Brunswick, then ties it up again and hands it to Sam. "Will you wear it in today's game? Who's going to know the difference? Your teammates admire you and will follow you anywhere. And if the school district complains, we'll say, 'There's no rules about wearing a Canadian Provincial Flag on your arm. So, sue us!' Will you be captain? At least for one big game?"

Sam pauses to savor the moment, then says, "I'm ready. Win or lose, I say, 'Let's breathe some dragon fire this afternoon!'"

He ties the cloth securely around his upper arm. Maddie runs up and hugs him and kisses his cheek, then steps away. Nana steps up and says, "I got one of those too!" and kisses him on the cheek.

"Well, I've got to get ready for school and for the game too.

Maddie . . . we'll talk later! Nana will take you home. Thanks everyone for an amazing cool weekend, in the company of so many very special sentient beings. Especially you, Madeleine!"

Blushing, she says, "How'd you know my real name, Sam?"

"Lucky guess!"

When Nana drops Maddie off at her home, her parents are waiting outside, getting ready for another Monday at work. Sparks runs up to Maddie and jumps in her arms. After hugs and kisses and a lot of spontaneous pet therapy, they all go to the backyard.

"Mom, Dad, I have so much to tell you!" Maddie says breathlessly, for once unconcerned about how she is going to say things to avoid their negative reactions. She no longer feels she is stepping on eggshells.

"Maddie, we have something to tell you too," her mother says. "Something amazing has happened, Maddie," her father begins. "Remember the sickly Monarda plant in the backyard? We almost pulled it out, remember? Now look!"

The Monarda is loaded with red blossoms, and there are at least twenty dragonflies flying around it, with a dozen hummingbirds feeding on its nectar. A squirrel is looking down from a nearby tree and a chipmunk is peeking from behind a nearby bush. One dragonfly flies right up to Maddie, and she hears, "Look on the ground!"

She looks around on the grass, and there a few feet away is an Ambystoma macrodactylum, a Western long-toed salamander, looking right at her, showing off her golden stripe. Maddie hears its golden voice speaking to her telepathically. "It's a brand-new day! And your adventures have just begun, Maddie!"

AFTERWORD
QUESTIONS FOR REFLECTION

What amazes you about the natural world?

How do you feel when you're in nature, in the forest, or near the ocean?

Professor Schroom explains how trees "talk" to each other. How does this change the way you look at a forest?

Love the land and it will love you back. How does reciprocity, a cooperative give and take exchange, work in nature?

Nature is sentient. The book defines sentient as the capacity to see, feel, and perceive. How have you noticed this?

The more diverse an ecosystem is, the healthier it is. What does this mean for human beings?

What are you grateful for? How does it feel to be grateful?

Why is community vital?

What kind of preparedness is necessary in times of climate change?

Mother Tree shows Sam and Maddie how to go into their inner world. How can looking inward impact the outer world?

Sam is more logical and Maddie more intuitive. Why is it important to have both kinds of thinkers when solving problems like climate change?

What is the role of perspective in solving problems? What are the benefits of seeing things from another perspective?

What can we do to create the world that we want?

It takes courage to be a pioneer. What do you want to do as an earth and water protector? What are your gifts?

READERS RESPOND

Mare Cromwell

Author of *Messages From Mother . . . Earth Mother*

Woven into the fabric of this highly captivating book lies great spiritual wisdom. Although SilverLight's adventures as she dances in and out of various Realms of Possibility with Sam and Maddie may seem like a fairy tale to many, those with visionary gifts know there is great truth being shared here.

This delightful story of two gifted children and their ecologically wise grandmother offers glimmers of insight which we yearn for during these stressful times. While people in Sam and Maddie's school are trying to plant seeds of doubt in their minds, the Mirror Dragon, an ambassador of Oneness, is busy planting seeds of hope for a New Earth filled with joy and love. Many young adults know they are here to help birth this New Earth. They will feel heartened and understood as they read of the 'magical' events in this story.

Here within our physical realms, the trees, chipmunks, owls, salamanders, and all the other sentient beings around us are calling for us to wake up and remember to take our rightful place as relative newcomers to the vast web of life we belong to. I am certain they are celebrating that Elizabeth Flanders has found the courage to write this book, with support from her assistant Evan Pritchard.

May many readers find themselves inspired intellectually and awakened spiritually by the deep wisdom and knowledge within this book, and may this wisdom usher in our beautiful future!

Pam Montgomery

Author of *Plant Spirit Healing: A Guide to Working with Plant Consciousness*

LIFE IS FILLED WITH MAGIC

I remember as a little girl visiting my Grandparents' farm in the eastern hills of Kentucky where I reveled in the beauty and magic of the natural world. There was a particular Pawpaw tree tucked in the corner next to the smokehouse where I would play. The branches were low hanging, and I could crawl underneath and be completely hidden from sight by any passers-by. This was my magical world where I would spend hours in play with the "little people" as I called them.

I loved my time under the Pawpaw tree, and at the time, this all felt quite normal until I told one of my cousins about the "little people". This was my first encounter with ridicule. I was shamed and told I was making it all up. I learned quickly not to talk with anyone about my adventures, and the times with the "little people" became part of my secret inner life.

When Elizabeth shared with me that she was writing her first book, *Sam, Maddie and the Mirror Dragon,* I was thrilled that she was willing to bring both her knowledge of the natural world and her abilities as a conduit for the more than human realms together in a lively story that speaks to our current ecological crisis.

As I read Elizabeth's book I was delighted when I came across this passage where the teenage protagonists, Sam and Maddie, met two fairy beings who said, "We are Songmaster

Souls. Our mission is to sing the New Earth into reality. On your present earth you would call us fairies."

"You are real! You are real! I knew you when I was little," exclaimed Maddie. "Mom and Dad said you weren't real, and I needed to grow up."

Once again, I was brought back to my time under the Pawpaw tree as if it was yesterday. What an affirmation to read these words and know I was not alone as a child! If only all little children and their openness to other dimensions and etheric beings could be respected and even encouraged, what a different world we would live in. Perhaps we would not be so separate from Nature.

As Sam and Maddie are transported back and forth between the "Realms of Possibilities" and their daily life of school, family and sports, a deep wisdom emerges where they are informed and guided by their non-human mentors to become earth and water protectors with effects on both their personal lives and the world at large.

As you dive into the world of Sam and Maddie you may feel as if you are drinking from a deep well of wisdom. You may remember a long-forgotten time when we were kin with all of nature including the more than human realm. What an exciting testament to all the possibilities that hold solutions not problems. This is a refreshingly unique view of New Earth, where magic is within our grasp!

Co-Creators

Elizabeth Flanders, M.A. Author

Elizabeth Flanders is a storyteller who believes the most powerful magic in the world is the kind we find in our own backyards. For many years she has experienced and observed the beauty and joy that comes with living in reciprocity, a cooperative give and take exchange, with the natural world.

Sam, Maddie and the Mirror Dragon grew out of Elizabeth's direct experience with young people, as a mother, grandmother and teacher of 40 years in widely diverse environments. This story is in response to their hunger for a deeper understanding of themselves and their place in our world.

Elizabeth is a passionate advocate for environmental literacy or understanding how Nature works and how we are a part of it all. In this fast-paced fantasy the characters experience how we are interconnected with the patterns in Nature that keep life on this planet alive and healthy. She believes that when young people learn to love Nature, they will naturally grow up to protect it.

Evan Prichard, Co-author, Editor and Illustrator

Evan's vision inspired our cover art. The inner illustrations for SilverLight and the Ent are his as well. A semi-retired college professor and writing workshop leader, Evan lives in the Hudson Valley in New York state and is the sole author of over fifty books and has edited and co-authored countless more on a wide range of topics. As a TV/magazine journalist, he conducted a number of interviews with the late Madeleine L'Engle, who developed the Young Adult novel to what it is today "and taught him all he knows". As a writing consultant, he has worked with CBS News, Oprah Winfrey, Bernie Siegel, Jean Houston, and many more.

Naeshi, Artist for Cover and all Other Inner Illustrations

Anne-Sophie Hilger, Naeshi on social media, is a young, self-taught French illustrator who enjoys drawing magical landscapes and people. She started drawing as soon as she picked up a pencil and has never stopped!

Diane Elliot, Sponsor, made this book possible.

Mayfly Design, Book Design and Publishing Services, brought it into the world.

ACKNOWLEDGMENTS

Deepest Gratitude and Love

To Diane Elliot, your vision and generosity made this book possible.

To Evan Prichard, gifted writer, illustrator, and editor supreme, it was a pleasure co-creating this book with you.

To Christie Vallance, you stood by my side through all the ups and downs.

To Danielle Elaine, Henrietta Haines, Danella Mauguin, and Haris Wolfgang, you lifted me up when I most needed it.

To Mare Cromwell and Pam Montgomery, for your inspiration, support, and facilitation.

To Naeshi, amazing artist, your illustrations bring the story alive.

To all of you who took the time to read the various drafts of this book. You know who you are.

To my family, Steven, Michaela, Jason, and Vincent, for your love and support.

And to Mother Earth and All My Relations, for you are the fertile ground from which this story grew.

Elizabeth Flanders

BIBLIOGRAPHY

Banyacya, Thomas, "The Legend of the Rainbow Warriors," https://theearthstoriescollection.org/en/the-legend-of-the-rainbow-warriors/.

Brach, Tara. "Resources: Working with Grief and Loss," last accessed October 14, 2022, Facebook https://www.tarabrach.com/grief/.

Burke Museum of Natural History and Culture, "Green Darner Dragonfly: Washington state insect," September 8, 2016, https://www.burkemuseum.org/news/green-darner-dragonfly-washington-state-insect.

Center for Whale Research, "A Bird's Eye View of Orcas," October 21, 2021, A bird's-eye view of orcas! How, when, and why? https://www.whaleresearch.com/.

Center for Whale Research, "Orca Identification," accessed October 26, 2022, Orca Identification, https://www.whaleresearch.com/.

College of the Environment University of Washington, "Fleet," accessed October 25, 2022, Fleet | College of the Environment, https://www.washington.edu/.

Davidson, Jordan, "40 Percent of World's Plants at Risk of Extinction, New Report Finds," EcoWatch, accessed September 30, 2020, https://www.ecowatch.com/.

Deep Green Permaculture, "The Complete Guide to Worm Farming, Vermicomposting Made Easy," accessed October 19, 2022, The Complete Guide to Worm Farming, Vermicomposting Made Easy—Deep Green Permaculture.

Getten, Mary, "Communicating with Orcas—The Whale's Perspective," Smashwords Edition, 2014, Kindle.

Grant, Richard, "Do Trees Talk to Each Other," March 2018, https://www.smithsonianmag.com/science-nature/the-whispering-trees-180968084/.

Henningsen, Kristin, "Mycelium—What Is It and Why Is It So Important," February 27, 2020, https:ommushrooms.com/blogs/blog/what-is-mycelium.

Hetherington, Alistair, "Guard Cells," August 07, 2001, https://www.cell.com/current-biology/fulltext/S0960-9822(01)00358-X.

Hopwood, Octavia, "The Rhizosphere: an interaction between soil roots and biology," June 7, 2017 59degrees YouTube, The Rhizosphere: an interaction between plant roots and soil biology—YouTube.

Know Your Forest, "Oregon White Oak and Wildlife.pdf," 2018, https://www.knowyourforest.org/.

Lagomarsino, Valentina, "Exploring the Underground Network of Trees—The Nervous System of the Forest," accessed October 23, 2022, Exploring The Underground Network of Trees—The Nervous System of the Forest—Science in the News, https://www.harvard.edu/.

Lotzof, Kerry, "Natural History Museum, accessed October 10, 2022, Are we really made of stardust? | Natural History Museum, https://www.nhm.ac.uk/.

National Park Service, "Douglas Squirrel," accessed October 17, 2022, https://www.nps.gov/articles/000/douglas-s-squirrel.htm.

National Resources Defense Council, "Regenerative Agriculture 101," November 29, 2021, Regenerative Agriculture 101 | NRDC.

Norman, Calvin and Kreye, Melissa, "How Forests Store Carbon," updated September 24, 2020, PennState Extension, How Forests Store Carbon, https://www.psu.edu/.

Nova season 47 episode 10, "Secret Mind of Slime," September 16, 2020.

Nunez, Christina, "Deforestation Explained," accessed October 19, 2022, Deforestation, facts and information, https://www.nationalgeographic.com/.

Phillpots, Eden, "The universe is full of magic things waiting for our senses to grow sharper," https://quoteinvestigator.com/2012/07/07/magical-things-waiting.

Psychology Today, "Forest Bathing," accessed November 4, 2022, Forest Bathing | Psychology Today.

Randall at Spirit Animal Totems, "Chipmunk," December 21, 2021, Chipmunk Symbolism, Dreams, and Messages—Spirit Animal Totems https://www.spirit-animals.com/.

Seeger, Pete, "My Dirty Stream (The Pete Seeger Hudson River Song)," January 17, 1966, Track #14 on God Bless the Grass, Columbia Records, vinyl.

Smithsonian, *The Tree Book: the stories, science, and history of trees,* (New York: DK Publishing, 2022).

Spirit Animal Dreams, "Seagull Spirit Animal Symbolism and Dreams," last accessed October 15, 2022, SEAGULL SPIRIT ANIMAL—Symbolism & Dreams, https://www .spiritanimaldreams.com/.

Timreck, Ted, "The Great Falls version 1: dated September 21, 2021, https://youtu.be/hN_uMuiHBGM.

The Salish Sea School, "Dave Ellifrit, Researcher, Photo ID Specialist," May 11, 2020, RESEARCH—Orca Photo ID Specialist!—YouTube.

Wikipedia, "Flame Skimmer," accessed October 30, 2022, Flame Skimmer—Wikipedia.

NOTES

1. Burke Museum of Natural History and Culture, "Green Darner Dragonfly: Washington state insect," September 8, 2016, https://www.burkemuseum.org/news/green-darner-dragonfly -washington-state-insect.
2. "Oregon White Oak and Wildlife," 2018, Oregon White Oak and Wildlife.pdf, https://www.knowyourforest.org/.
3. Temreck, Ted, "The Great Falls," version 1: dated September 21, 2021, https://youtu.be/hN_uMuiHBGM.
4. "Flame Skimmer," Wikipedia accessed October 30, 2022, Flame skimmer—Wikipedia.
5. Brach, Tara, "Resources: Working with Grief and Loss," last accessed October 14, 2022, Facebook https://www.tarabrach.com/grief/.
6. Grant, Richard, "Do Trees Talk to Each Other," March 2018, https://www.smithsonianmag.com/science-nature/the -whispering-trees-180968084/.
7. "Seagull Spirit Animal Symbolism and Dreams," last accessed October 15, 2022, SEAGULL SPIRIT ANIMAL—Symbolism & Dreams, https://www.spiritanimaldreams.com.
8. Eden Phillpots, "A Shadow Passes, New York, MacMIllan 1919, reprinted Neuilly sur Seine France by Ulan Press, 2012.
9. Smithsonian, The Tree Book: the stories, science, and history of trees, (New York: DK Publishing, 2022), 18-19.
10. Hetherington, Alistar, "Guard Cells," August 07, 2001, https: //www.cell.com/current-biology/fulltext/S0960-9822(01)00358-X.
11. Zion.Klos P., Mother Nature's Hit Single: https://ui.adsabs.harvard .edu or google "mother nature's hit single" sdf https://ui.adsabs .harvard.edu › abs › abstract.
12. https://www.bing.com/search?q=Pete%20Seeger&FORM= SNAPST.

13. Seeger, Pete, "My Dirty Stream (The Pete Seeger Hudson River Song)," January 17, 1966, track # 14 on God Bless the Grass, Columbia Records, vinyl. Los Angeles, Sangha Music.

14. "Forest Bathing," Psychology Today accessed November 4, 2022, Forest Bathing | Psychology Today.

15. Nova season 47 episode 10, "Secret Mind of Slime," September 16, 2020.

16. National Park Service, "Douglas Squirrel," accessed October 17, 2022, https://www.nps.gov/articles/000/douglas-s-squirrel.htm.

17. Deep Green Permaculture, "The Complete Guide to Worm Farming, Vermicomposting Made Easy," accessed October 19, 2022, The Complete Guide to Worm Farming, Vermicomposting Made Easy—Deep Green Permaculture.

18. Nunez, Christina, "Deforestation Explained," accessed October 19, 2022, Deforestation, facts and information, https://www.nationalgeographic.com/.

19. Norman, Calvin and Kreye, Melissa, "How Forests Store Carbon," updated September 24, 2020, PennState Extension, How Forests Store Carbon, https://www.psu.edu/.

20. Davidson, Jordan, "40 Percent of World's Plants at Risk of Extinction, New Report Finds," EcoWatch, September 30, 2020, accessed October 19, 2022, https://www.ecowatch.com/plants-biodiversity-extinction-2647868027.html.

21. Banyacya, Thomas, "The Legend of the Rainbow Warriors," https://theearthstoriescollection.org/en/the-legend-of-the-rainbow-warriors/.

22. Henningsen, Kristin, "Mycelium—What Is It and Why Is It So Important," February 27, 2020, https:ommushrooms.com/blogs/blog/what-is-mycelium.

23. Lagomarsino, Valentina, "Exploring the Underground Network of Trees—The Nervous System of the Forest," accessed October 23, 2022, Exploring The Underground Network of Trees—The Nervous System of the Forest—Science in the News, https://www.harvard.edu/.

24. Hopwood, Octavia, "The Rhizosphere: an interaction between soil roots and biology," June 7, 2017 59degrees YouTube, The Rhizosphere: an interaction between plant roots and soil biology—YouTube.

25. National Resources Defense Council, "Regenerative Agriculture 101," November 29, 2021, Regenerative Agriculture 101 | NRDC.

26. https://en.wikipedia.org/wiki/Captain_(association_football)

27. https://www.weforum.org/agenda/2022/09/transparent-solar -panel-windows/

28. https://www.robinwallkimmerer.com/

29. https://www.nps.gov/subjects/tek/description.htm

30. College of the Environment University of Washington, "Fleet," accessed October 25, 2022, Fleet | College of the Environment, https://www.washington.edu/.

31. The Salish Sea School, "Dave Ellifrit, Researcher, Photo ID Specialist, May 11, 2020, RESEARCH—Orca Photo ID Specialist!—YouTube.

32. https://en.wikipedia.org/wiki/Michael_Bigg.

33. Center for Whale Research, "Orca Identification," accessed October 26, 2022, Orca Identification, https://www .whaleresearch.com/.

34. Center for Whale Research, "Orca Identification," accessed October 26, 2022, Orca Identification, https://www .whaleresearch.com/.

35. Center for Whale Research, "Orca Identification," accessed October 26, 2022, Orca Identification, https://www .whaleresearch.com/.

36. Getten, Mary, J., "Communicating with Orcas—The Whale's Perspective," Smashwords Edition, 2014, page 374, Kindle.

37. https://www.montananaturalist.org/blog-post/avian-adaptations/.

38. A Bird's Eye View of Orcas, October 21, 2021, A bird's-eye view of orcas! How, when, and why? https://www.whaleresearch.com/.

39. Getten, Mary, J., "Communicating with Orcas—The Whale's Perspective," Smashwords Edition, 2014, page 836, Kindle.

40. https://www.climate.gov/news-features/understanding-climate/
climate-change-global-sea-level.
41. Getten, Mary J., "Communicating with Orcas—The Whale's
Perspective," Smashwords Edition, 2014, page 609, Kindle.
42. "Chipmunk," Spirit Animal Totems and the messages they
bring you," Randall, December 21, 2021, Chipmunk Symbolism,
Dreams, and Messages—Spirit Animal Totems, https://www
.spiritanimaldreams.com.

Sam, Maddie, and the Mirror Dragon,

by first time Pacific Northwest author Elizabeth Flanders, with assistance from veteran New York writer and illustrator Evan Pritchard, is a story in the tradition of young adult fantasy. Its dual 14-year-old protagonists Sam and Maddie, neighbors in a rural town in Washington state, (similar to where Elizabeth lives) are drawn unexpectedly into The Mother Tree's powerful vortex, and find a portal where they meet SilverLight, a thousands-years-old master dragon, who begins to teach them Mother Earth's Secrets as no mere mortal could. To train the two teens to become Galactic Guardian-Level Earth-Protectors, SilverLight magically transports them back and forth between the everyday world of school and family and the various Realms of Possibilities that exist in other dimensions. A unique blend of natural and supernatural, this inspirational and highly educational novel provides up-to-date information about the environmental dangers facing young adults today and what they can do to respond as Earth- and Water-Protectors.